Paul's eyes sw
angular shad
then began to
ing, a wooden strut or something. Then it moved,
fleshing itself out into a human figure. He blinked
hard. You could make yourself see anything in the
dark.

He wasn't certain, but he couldn't ignore his
instincts. "Sam?" He called out the name softly.

Why was he running away? Paul could see the
dark figure, now far ahead of him, crisscrossing
the alley, leaping from rooftop to rooftop in huge,
weightless strides.

"Hey!" he panted. "Sam, that you?"

The slim figure crouched at the end of the
pier, facing the water. Paul's heart jumped.

"Sam," he said, walking closer, feeling such
relief.

Sam turned around to face him, but it wasn't
Sam.

DEAD WATER ZONE

Kenneth Oppel

An Imprint of HarperCollinsPublishers

Eos is an imprint of HarperCollins Publishers.

Dead Water Zone
Copyright © 1992 by Kenneth Oppel,
© 2001 by Firewing Productions, Inc.

For information address HarperCollins Children's Books,
a division of HarperCollins Publishers,
1350 Avenue of the Americas, New York, NY 10019.
www.harperteen.com

Library of Congress Cataloging-in-Publication Data
Oppel, Kenneth, 1967-
    Dead water zone / Kenneth Oppel. — 1st Eos paperback ed.
        p.   cm.
    Summary: Muscular sixteen-year-old Paul tries to find his
genetically stunted younger brother Sam in the polluted ruins of
Watertown, where Sam is trying to cure himself with toxic "dead
water" that alters the metabolism of those who drink it.
    ISBN 978-0-06-123442-2 (pbk.)
    [1. Brothers—Fiction. 2. Science fiction.] I. Title.
PZ7.O614De 2007   2007011669
[Fic]—dc22   CIP
                                                   AC

Typography by Larissa Lawrynenko
❖
First Eos paperback edition, 2007
First published in paperback in Canada by HarperCollins Publishers Ltd., 2001
First published in hardcover in Canada by Kids Can Press, 1992

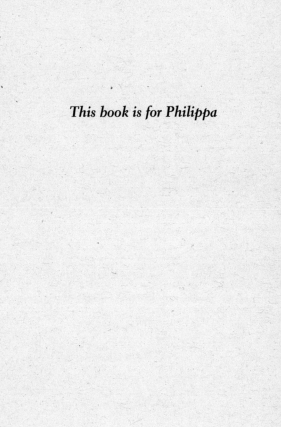

This book is for Philippa

DEAD
WATER
ZONE

1

PAUL DREAMED machinery.

The oiled push of steel pistons, the rustle of rubber hosing, the low roar of a powerful furnace.

He walked into his brother's room. Sam sat on the edge of the bed, curling barbells in toward his chest—right arm, left arm, one, two. Impossible. Sam was too weak to be lifting them.

"I'm getting stronger," Sam said. One, two, one, two, effortless.

"But how?" Paul asked.

"Secrets are subatomic," Sam replied with an enigmatic smile.

"What does that mean?" Paul demanded. How typical of Sam to say something clever and not explain it. "What does that mean?"

"Look."

Sam lowered the barbells to the floor and began peeling off his layers of clothing, one sweatshirt, then another, then another—all the time getting skinnier and skinnier.

"You don't have to do this," Paul said anxiously. "You don't have to, Sam. Stop!"

But Sam kept stripping off his shirts, until he came to the very last one. Paul knew what was underneath.

"Don't!" he shouted. "Sam, please, I'm sorry!"

"Paul," his brother said, "watch."

There was a blinding flash of skeletal white, but something else, too, something metallic.

"No!" Paul shouted. "No, no, no!"

He clamped his eyes shut, but the scalding brightness filled his dream vision, white and intense as a camera's flash, then slowly faded to the dark color of deep water.

2

THE SMALL motorboat humped across the water.
Paul felt every wave through the thin metal
hull, as if they were riding over a corrugated rib
cage. He wasn't used to boats, and he didn't feel
particularly safe in this one. The oily pool quivering at his shoes had expanded since they'd started
out. And once, when he'd looked back over his
shoulder at the pilot, he'd seen him scooping up
some water with an old coffee mug and flinging it
hurriedly over the side. Paul grimaced. He'd been
too eager; he'd just hopped into the first boat he'd
seen for hire.

He could make out Watertown's low sprawl in
the distance now, the vast shantytown suspended
on a rickety webwork of pilings and piers. He'd

seen pictures, but he'd never traveled down here before. He didn't know anyone who had. If his parents found out—but they wouldn't. That part had been easy. He hadn't even lied, not really.

He couldn't help feeling a sense of accomplishment. Everything so far had gone off smoothly: the commuter train from Governor's Hill through the Outer Neighborhoods, then the stinking subway, which had slung him down into the City and dumped him at the docklands. From there, boat was the only way. He glanced at his watch. Still plenty of time.

There was a sudden tightness across his chest, and he felt short of breath. He told himself he'd been sitting too long, letting his muscles cramp; he told himself he was getting out of shape. But he knew it was nervousness. Push-ups. That always did the trick. Got the body working again. He flexed the powerful muscles in his thighs and upper arms and felt vaguely reassured.

He could see the outer reaches of Watertown clearly now. Boats dotted the water—small blackened things, some no bigger than oversized bathtubs with motors. Decrepit houseboats were tied up along spidery jetties. Tar paper shacks lined the higher wharves, dark tendrils of smoke lifting from tin-can roofs. Paul felt a knot forming in his guts.

The motorboat swung in and bumped up

against the tires nailed to one of the jetties.

"How much do I owe you?"

"Fifty."

He should have asked the price before they left. He was getting taken, but he didn't have it in him to haggle. He could already hear his voice trembling with uncertainty. He hated scenes. Forget it, he told himself. He yanked out the bills. It didn't leave a lot. He handed the money to the pilot, hefted the knapsack onto his shoulder, and stepped clumsily from the rocking boat, nearly losing his balance.

He took a few angry steps across the jetty before remembering to ask for directions. But when he turned, the boat was heading back to the docklands.

"Thanks for everything," Paul muttered. It didn't matter, he told himself. He had plenty of time. He'd find the way on his own.

He wasn't prepared for the number of people. There must have been hundreds in plain view, men and women and kids scraping at overturned hulls, pumping fuel from ancient gas machines, pushing wheelbarrows filled with potatoes and withered lettuce. People sat idly on the edge of the dock, smoking, talking; others marched along erratically, arms churning, shouting to themselves.

Paul felt something approaching panic. You

didn't get people like this on the streets in Governor's Hill. You stepped out the front door and into the car. If you had a garage, you didn't even need to go outside. The mall—that was the only place you saw lots of people. But even then, there was an orderliness to it, a purposefulness. There were rules.

What a stink! His nostrils wrinkled in revulsion. His world was odorless, anything offensive conjured away by jets of recirculating air. But here he felt instantly filthy, overwhelmed by rank body odor, unwashed clothing, the funk of rotting vegetables and fish.

All at once, he was painfully conscious of his own clothing: the new track shoes, the white T-shirt that gleamed amid the drab, washed-out colors around him. Worst of all was his knapsack—a bright, crayon red.

A flush of embarrassment was working its way up his back into his armpits. There were so many eyes on him. He felt like a robot from a low-budget science fiction film, stiff legs jerking out, one, two, one, two. He wished he could just fade in. He caught another glimpse of his shiny sneakers. What a disaster. At least he could have scuffed them up a little, trudged through a puddle or something.

A man with blue spider tattoos across his face

sidled past, almost nudging. Paul swallowed, his body tensed. He was glad he was big. He weighed in at over 175. And he looked older than sixteen, everyone said so. Most of the people here looked skinny, underfed. Still, if a lot of them banded together . . .

Wharves and jetties shot off in all directions, creating an intricate web of canals, some so narrow that you could jump across, others wide enough for sleek boats to navigate.

He looked for signposts. There were none. He realized he'd been carrying in his head a ridiculous image of neat, suburban streets, marked at every corner. A name—that was all he had to go on, the name of a pier. But how many piers were there? Hundreds, thousands?

He'd have to ask directions. He saw a woman sitting in the doorway of a shack, her head bent over a book. She looked all right; she'd give him directions. He came closer. The book was a tattered department store catalog. Her fingers flipped spasmodically through the pages.

"Excuse me—"

The woman lifted her face to him, and Paul saw her mad eyes.

"I should have gotten the position," she said fiercely. "They underestimated me. They didn't realize how good my qualifications were. They know nothing, nothing! I should have gotten that position."

Nodding awkwardly, he backed away. She was shaking her head, spitting out words. He wanted to turn around and go home. It was a stinking madhouse! What could Sam be doing in a place like this?

A group of children had gathered around him, and a few moved in close, their small, curious hands brushing his clothing, then suddenly darted away, as if frightened.

Then he heard it, too. The dull thumping became a roar as an unmarked helicopter slewed through the air. It slowed and rotated overhead, hovering like an insistent insect. Paul kept going. The helicopter floated lazily along to one side, as if keeping pace with him. For a few panicky seconds, he wondered if it might be police, sent by his parents. But he knew it couldn't be. Besides, it wasn't a police helicopter.

A rock struck soundlessly against the machine's underbelly. Moments later, the helicopter veered up and away and was gone.

It was a few minutes before Paul felt confident enough to try for directions again. He saw a gaunt man perched on a crooked wooden pole, weaving a wire into a tangle of electrical cables. Stealing power. Paul could hear the ominous hum of the overloaded transformer.

"Jailer's Pier?" he asked hopefully. "Can you tell me how I get there?"

The man's eyes narrowed suspiciously.

"Jailer's?" he asked belligerently.

"Yes."

"What d'you want to go over there for?"

"I'm looking for someone," Paul said nervously.

"Ain't no one there."

The man turned away as if their conversation had reached an end.

"Look, do you know the way?"

The man hawked disdainfully into the water.

"Suit yourself." He pointed.

He was lost.

The jetties were closed in on both sides by abandoned shacks, bolted sloppily together from splintered planks and rusted sheets of corrugated metal. Sometimes he lost sight of the water altogether. But all he had to do was stand still and he could feel the lake's sway beneath his feet.

He'd told his parents he was going to stay with Sam. Of course, they'd assumed he meant at the university. They were probably only half listening anyway.

The alleys narrowed even further. He was lost, and now he was losing the light. Sam would snicker if he knew. Sam could have given him directions, sent a map, something! What was this, some ridiculous test? A game? Or maybe, thought Paul, he just doesn't want to see me.

Deep shadows seeped across the alley. He was desperate for directions now; he'd ask anyone. He'd even fork out another fifty. But he'd seen very few people in the last quarter of an hour. Ain't no one there, the gaunt man had said. He was supposed to be meeting Sam in ten minutes! How long would Sam wait? What if he left? How would he find him again in this place?

He started walking more quickly. There were no streetlamps; he hadn't known it could be this dark at night. His scalp prickled—he felt he was being watched. He glanced over his shoulder and thought of the helicopter. But his mind was already conjuring up other dangers, horrifying encounters around this corner, then the next. Faces looming out at him from hidden doorways, sudden cackles of laughter in his ear. How had he let it get so late?

Creaks and groans rose up from the planking beneath his feet. He was turning the sounds into footfalls, heavy breathing. He broke into a jog, the knapsack slapping against his back. There was someone following him, someone just out of sight, someone right behind him!

He couldn't bear it any longer. He whirled on the balls of his feet. No one. You're freaking, he told himself angrily. You're doing this to yourself.

But he couldn't silence the alarm that played in his head. He swallowed, feeling the sweat cooling against his skin, then tilted his face up. Something had just moved back from the roof's edge. He ran.

Ahead of him, a dark shape leaped across the alley to the opposite rooftop and was swallowed up in darkness. Paul slowed down. He didn't want to go too close. He didn't want anything jumping on his head. It could have been a bird or a large cat. It had seemed bigger, though, with a more human shape. That might have just been his imagination playing with the lines. Whatever it was, it was fast.

His eyes swept the rooflines, stopping at a long, angular shadow. He watched it for a long time and then began to relax. It was only part of the building, a wooden strut or something. Then it moved, fleshing itself out into a human figure. He blinked hard. You could make yourself see anything in the dark.

He wasn't certain, but he couldn't ignore his instincts. "Sam?" He called out the name softly.

The shape jerked back from the roof's edge. Paul ran down the alley after it, pushing himself hard.

"Sam?"

Why was he running away? Paul could see the dark figure, now far ahead of him, crisscrossing the alley, leaping from rooftop to rooftop in huge, weightless strides. It couldn't be Sam! At the end of the alley he caught another glimpse of it. Waiting for me to catch up, Paul thought. Was that it? He jogged closer. Still the figure didn't move.

"Hey!" he panted. "Sam, that you?"

The figure kept slipping in and out of shadow. Then it took a few steps back, made a running start, and jumped. The night swallowed it up.

Paul swore and charged ahead, but the alley dead-ended at a broad canal, separating him from the buildings on the far side. He dumped his knapsack to the ground and bent over to catch his breath.

Then he saw the slim figure crouched at the end of the pier, facing the water.

Paul's heart jumped.

"Sam," he said, walking closer, feeling such relief.

Sam turned around to face him, but it wasn't Sam.

3

WHAT HE NOTICED first about her was the pallor of her skin. Her narrow face almost seemed to gleam in the darkness. A shadowy mane of curly hair was pulled back from her forehead and gathered in a careless braid. She wore several baggy sweatshirts and canvas pants lined with clasped pockets. Bone-thin wrists and long, tapered hands poked through the cuffs of the army-surplus overcoat that hung loosely about her.

Paul stepped nervously back.

"Sorry. From behind you looked—"

He could feel the pinprick of her eyes slowly summing him up. He thought he saw the trace of a smile. So pale, there was something almost vampiric about her.

"So you thought I was someone else," she said. Her voice was languid with a softly sarcastic edge. No fangs at least.

Paul nodded awkwardly. His words spilled out to fill the silence.

"We were supposed to meet. At Jailer's Pier."

The girl held her hands aloft in an exaggerated shrug. "This is it. And here I am. Ain't no one else."

"This is Jailer's Pier?" He couldn't believe it—a complete fluke. "You didn't see anybody; you're sure?"

"No one lives around here. It's deserted."

"Listen," he said, trying to sound firm, "I saw someone—"

"Wasn't me, pal," she broke in, shaking her head.

"I was following him. He was running on the roofs, fast, and it was like he jumped right across that—" He jerked his head at the canal and the looming buildings on the far side.

The girl stiffened. "You saw someone go in there?"

Paul hesitated. Looking at the canal, he saw that it was very wide. Surely no one could jump that! The buildings opposite formed a dark, unbroken wall.

"It looked like it. He jumped—the light's no

14

good; how could I tell really?"

She turned away with a dismissive grunt. "Shadow play maybe," she muttered. "You get weird shapes on the water at night. Seen them myself a hundred times. Doesn't mean anything."

He felt chastised. Maybe he'd just wanted it to be Sam, and his mind's eye had done the rest.

"But there was someone," he mumbled. There was no mistaking that much.

"Who were you supposed to meet?"

"My brother."

Her eyebrows arched slightly. "And he's ditched you here, the middle of Watertown?"

"It seems so."

"Nice brother." She muttered something else, shaking her head. What a fool he must seem.

"No place to stay, right?" she said.

Her question caught him off guard. He'd just assumed he would meet Sam, and something would be worked out. But the girl was right—he was stranded.

"I don't suppose you could recommend someplace nearby. A reasonable motel?" He forced a smile. It was the best he could do, given the circumstances.

"You'll get taken apart if you stay out here," she said without much concern.

"Oh."

"You'd better come with me. There's a place you can stay. One night, no more."

Paul didn't want to take his chances alone in Watertown, huddled in some empty shack.

"Yeah, thanks," he said. After a moment's hesitation, he added, "I'm Paul Berricker." He took a step forward, his hand half extended, but when she made no similar move, he let the hand fall to his side, embarrassed.

"Monica Shanks," the girl said.

As he hefted his red knapsack, she gave a low laugh. "You look like a cartoon."

Armitage Shanks was almost as skinny as his sister, with the same pale skin and piercing eyes. He wore baggy cotton trousers and a black tank top, beneath which Paul could make out the contours of his rib cage. His bare arms were slender, but they had definition—the small, hard bulge of biceps, low hump of the triceps. His jet-black hair was scraped neatly back from his face into a short ponytail. There was a small tattoo of a schooner on his forearm. Paul imagined him with an eye patch, a belt and cutlass slung around his narrow hips.

"Long way down from Governor's Hill," said Armitage, wiping sweat from his forehead. Behind him, four other teenagers unloaded crates from the old cabin cruiser tied up inside the boathouse. "How'd you get across from the docklands?"

"Water taxi."

Armitage smiled. "How much did you pay?"

Paul chewed at his lower lip sheepishly.

"Fifty. I got ripped off, I suppose, didn't I?"

"Oh yeah. So, is this a family outing? Should we expect your parents soon?"

The tone was amiable, even playful, but Paul could see the bright spark of suspicion in the other boy's eyes. All those cardboard crates, stacked up against the walls. He didn't want to know about it.

"I came alone."

"He brought a big red knapsack," said Monica, slouched against the wall. "Like he was planning on staying awhile."

"Yes, I can see the knapsack," said Armitage. "It's a fine knapsack. You can probably fit a lot into a knapsack like that. Lunch box, coloring book, crayons—the works."

Paul forced a grin. He wished he'd left the damn knapsack at home.

"Do they know you came here, your mommy and daddy?" Armitage inquired with a contemptuous twang.

"No, nobody knows."

"Good." Armitage scratched his nose distractedly. "Last thing we need is hysterical suburban parents trying to send half the police force in here to rescue their son. There's only one other thing that bugs me, Paul," he confided. "Let me tell you a story. Once, the police tried to set us up. They got some kid, some nobody punk, to come down here and say he needed a place to stay. When we found out what he really wanted, he ended up swimming back to the docklands."

Paul shrugged, meeting Armitage's gaze evenly. "That's not why I came," he said. He turned to Monica. "Look, forget it. I didn't think it was going to be such a big hassle. I'll just take my knapsack and—"

"Hey, Paul, come on!" Armitage said with a disarming smile. "We're just giving you a hard time. I was getting to know you. I'm in a trusting mood tonight." He opened his arms magnanimously. "Don't you trust him, Monica?"

She shrugged, noncommittal. "I said he could stay one night."

"See, we both trust you, Paul."

Paul couldn't help smiling. They trusted him. Great. They were probably the most untrustworthy people he'd ever met.

"I'm happy to have you stay with us," Armitage said warmly. Paul expected him to throw an arm around his shoulder at any moment. "So, this brother of yours, he didn't show, huh?"

"He said he'd meet me. I don't know what happened."

They'd arranged the time, the place; so why hadn't Sam been there? What had stopped him?

"What'd he do, run away from home?"

"Yes," Paul lied. He wanted to tell them as little as possible. "I think he came down three or four weeks ago. I'm not sure."

"What's his name?" Monica asked.

"Samuel Berricker. Sam."

Armitage narrowed his eyes, as if thinking hard, but shook his head. "Haven't heard of him."

"A lot of people live here without showing themselves," said Monica. "You can still be invisible in Watertown."

"Look," said Paul, "I've got a picture."

He reached into his back pocket and his stomach plunged. His wallet was gone. He hurriedly patted all his other pockets, but it was no use. Now this, on top of everything else. His ID, the rest of his money, the photograph—gone. What a hell of a day.

"Pickpockets," Monica said sympathetically. "The place is overrun with them."

"Those little kids," he said, suddenly remembering. "They pressed up close—"

"They didn't pickpocket you," Monica said easily. "I did." She held out his wallet.

Paul was too surprised to feel any anger.

"Just making sure you're who you say you are. Nothing personal."

"Yeah. Right." He was at a complete loss for words. "So, you're a pickpocket."

"It's a job," she replied. "At least it's a skilled trade."

"She's very good," Armitage said.

"I didn't feel a thing," said Paul. His eyes rested on her slender hands, half expecting them to dart back into his pockets at any moment. "Is it a good living?"

"That's such a suburban question," Monica snorted. "It's not bad. And I know the next question you want to ask. The answer's no, I don't feel guilty."

Paul could only stare.

"I mostly go into the City," she went on. "They can afford it. I try to stick to the suits. Anyone else is a waste of time really. I never do credit cards. That's sleazy. All I take is the cash. If they're carrying hard currency around, they can afford to lose it. It might be a little upsetting to them at first, but they get over it."

Paul turned helplessly to Armitage. "So, what about you?"

Grinning, Armitage jerked his head at the activity behind him.

"Right, right," Paul mumbled. "I guess neither of you go to school, huh?"

"No time," said Monica. "Too much work to be done." She dangled his watch between her fingers.

"All right," said Paul, snatching it back. "I get the point."

"This is the last," called out one of the boys, hefting a crate onto a tall stack.

It looked like hard work and these guys were all so skinny and pale. Shouldn't they have been tanned, with all the sunlight off the water? Maybe it was too much night work, Paul thought wryly.

"Good work, guys," said Armitage. "Let's lock it up."

Outside, Monica and Armitage guided him along the pier to a ramshackle stilt house set back from the edge of the pier. Its bottom floor began well above Paul's head. Two small boats were tethered among the web of stilts and scaffolding.

Armitage started up a frail ladder. When he reached the top, he fiddled with a padlock, pushed open the door, and disappeared inside. Lights flickered on behind the windows.

"You better let me take the knapsack," Monica said.

"It's okay, I can manage."

"You don't get it," she said. "I don't want you

21

busting the ladder."

Before he could object, she'd slipped the knapsack off his shoulder and danced up the wooden rungs.

As Paul took his first step, the whole ladder seemed to go rigid with stress. Not meant for big people, he thought. Just as well she'd taken the knapsack. He glanced down and saw the dark water, waiting for him. He decided not to look down again and soon scuttled gratefully inside.

He'd expected squalor. Instead there were rugs everywhere, not only on the floor but on the walls, too. Ornate tapestries had somehow been fastened overhead—staples, nails?—and billowed down slightly in the middle, so the whole ceiling was an enormous pillowy quilt of red and gold. There were so many intricate designs in the room that Paul felt dizzy.

"Beats staring at boards," said Monica, letting her body slide, with feline grace, into a tattered armchair. She made, Paul noticed, only the slightest of depressions in the cushion.

As he walked into the center of the room, the floor creaked ominously beneath his feet, and he had a sudden vision of the stilt house as a dilapidated wooden shell, sagging in on itself. But it didn't change the bizarre grandeur of the place.

"You live here all alone?" he asked, and

immediately wished he hadn't. Monica's face hardened, and he could see the mocking glint in Armitage's eyes.

"What you mean is, where's Mom and Dad?"

Paul faltered. "Well—"

"It seems they are not at home," sneered Monica.

"And haven't been for, oh, quite a long time now," said Armitage. "Don't worry, Paul, we eat and wash regularly. We even floss our teeth sometimes."

Paul decided to shut up. No school, no parents—he was a coddled child who knew nothing of the world. They didn't teach you things like this in Governor's Hill.

"So, show us this brother of yours," Armitage said.

Paul pulled the snapshot from his wallet.

After looking at it a long time, Armitage shook his head. "Nope."

"Let me see." Monica pulled the photograph from her brother's fingers. "He doesn't look much like you."

"No."

"What's wrong with him?"

Paul felt himself tighten inside.

"It's a metabolic thing," he explained tersely. "He was born with it."

"That why he's so small?"

"Yes. He didn't grow right. His body's weak. He'll never get any bigger than that. But he's smart—a genius actually." He felt he needed to tell them, out of loyalty.

"Older or younger?" she wanted to know.

"A year younger."

"And a genius, huh?" She handed back the snapshot. "I've seen him."

"You have?" His voice broke with excitement. "Where?"

"One of the old boathouses off Nostromo Pier," she said in a bored voice. "I've seen him around there a few times, a couple of days ago even."

"Never told me," Armitage remarked, looking at her strangely.

She shrugged. "Why would I?"

"Can you take me?" Paul asked urgently. "Right now?"

She shook her head. "You can only get there by boat. And night's no good. There's too much junk in the water around there, stuff that'll take an engine right out. We'll have to wait until morning."

Paul tried to rein in his disappointment.

"She's right," Armitage told him. "You'll have to wait."

"He won't be going anywhere, either," Monica said, not unkindly. "I'll take you out at first light."

"Thanks," Paul said.

"You're tired, right?" said Armitage. "Big trip from Governor's Hill. New sights, new people. Come on, I'll show you where you can crash."

He stripped down to his underwear and began to exercise. It was an unbroken ritual—ten minutes before bed. And now, he also did it for comfort. He was in a strange place, about to lie down on a mattress of unknown origin, in a stilt house occupied by thieves. He finished his warm-up stretches and began his sit-ups, the wood floor creaking softly beneath him. Now the push-ups—gut sucked in, nose touching, twenty-eight, twenty-nine, thirty. There. That felt better.

Body singing, he slid his underwear off and stood before the tall, cracked mirror tilted against the wall. He planted his feet wide, straightened his arms at his sides, then slowly raised them so that they were level with his shoulders, then raised them again so that they were at an angle with his neck.

He gazed at his reflection, studying the lines of his body. He'd worked hard for it. Hours after school, laboring at the Universal Gym—that gave him muscle mass. Then the training for the track team, running, swimming—that gave him tone, suppleness, stamina.

The perfect man, perfectly proportioned. It was Sam who had shown him Leonardo da Vinci's famous sketch: a man inscribed in a circle and a square, striking this same pose. Sam could name every bone in the human body, every tangle of muscle, sinew, and vein. Sam, whose own body would only ever be weak and small. My younger brother. My genius brother.

Chest heaving, Paul let his arms fall back to his sides. Why had Sam come to this place? Think it through, he told his reflection. Go through the steps again.

Sam had won early entrance to the university last autumn. He'd been wasting his time in high school. Biochemistry and microbiology had become his passions. He'd done brilliantly in his first year, of course, and this summer he'd been offered a job as a research assistant at the laboratories, working for the City's new cleanup program.

The lake had been polluted for as long as Paul could remember. Even as a kid, there had been TV commercials by the City, advertising its cleanup program. Making Your City Shine Again. Glittering clear water, children splashing about, smiling faces.

DEAD WATER ZONE. Paul had seen a few of the warning buoys dotting the lake, marking out a perimeter around Watertown. In his letters, Sam said the City had been developing a microorganism that would break down the pollution. A garbage gobbler, he called it. Sam's job was to test water samples brought to the labs from around the lake.

Paul pulled his underwear back on and stretched out on the bed. The sheets seemed clean enough. He wedged his wallet under the pillow and stared up at the ceiling. It felt good to lie down. He could hear the sound of water, and he thought he felt the house rocking gently on its stilts—maybe it was just his body, still in motion after the long hours of traveling. He closed his eyes. Keep going through the steps.

The call came five days ago, his brother's voice wreathed in pay-phone static. They had talked awkwardly about everyday things. Then, in a sudden rush, Sam had told him he was in Watertown. He'd found something unusual in the water samples. No one else knew about it. He'd gone down himself to find out more. It was the only way. And then he said, "Something wonderful is going to happen."

Sam's voice was unbalanced, almost fanatical. What do you mean? Paul had asked. What are you talking about? But Sam was evasive. There was so much work to be done, he didn't have time to be talking on the phone. Paul kept insisting on the meeting until Sam agreed.

And he hadn't even shown up. Okay, maybe he'd changed his mind. But why Jailer's Pier? Impossible to find, completely deserted. Except for Monica. What was she doing there?

He was too tired. His thoughts were exploding away from him, dissolving. Everything would be all right. Tomorrow morning he'd see Sam and all his questions would be answered.

"How am I doing?" he panted.

While Sam checked his math homework, Paul did push-ups.

"Pretty good so far," his brother answered. "Only a couple of mistakes, but they were tricky ones. I'll pencil in the answers for you."

"Thanks. Word problems are the worst."

"How'd you do on your last test?"

"Twenty-two out of thirty."

"Hey, better than last time."

Sam was already two grades ahead of him. He could bring Sam any math problem, and his brother would just look at it for a few seconds and then scribble away, explaining as he went. Paul could ask him questions on any subject, and nine times out of ten, Sam would have the answer on the tip of his tongue. People sometimes asked him if he got jealous, having a brother who was a genius, but he was proud of Sam. And happy enough with his own marks. "Good solid work," one of his teachers had written on his report. Somehow it didn't matter if he didn't get brilliant marks, as long as Sam did. Marks were something they shared. Like Paul's muscles.

"Randy Smith was such a pain today," Sam remarked. "Thanks for thumping him for me."

"I like thumping Smith," Paul replied between push-ups. "If he hassles you again, we'll give him a working over."

"How many push-ups are you doing?"

"Fifty."

"The doctor gave me some new pills today."

"Yeah?"

"They look like hamster food."

Paul couldn't finish his last push-up, he was laughing so hard.

"But they're not as big as the last ones. I could hardly get those in my mouth! She says these should help me put on weight."

"They'll work," Paul answered confidently. "Pretty soon you'll be pumping iron, lifting cars, small buildings."

Sam chuckled. "I think I am getting stronger.

Last time we arm wrestled, I held out longer, didn't I?"

"You did," he said—convincingly, he hoped. The truth was, Sam seemed just the same, every time. Paul had to be very careful not to twist his pipe-cleaner wrist.

"When's your next track competition?"

"End of the month."

"Show me your muscles."

Paul stood and flexed his bare arms, watching his biceps harden, the veins swell. He liked doing this for Sam. To the right of his brother, he could see his own reflection in the mirror. But he must have stood up too quickly. For just a moment, as he glanced from Sam to the reflection and back, it seemed that his brother's head rested atop his muscular shoulders and his own body was suddenly frail and wizened.

He couldn't sleep. He was all wound up. With a sigh, he angled his watch face to the moonlight: 2:18. He stood, pacing the room, trying to relax. At the window he paused: a clear sky littered with stars and a half-moon reflected brilliantly in the black lake water. Someone was there, on the pier.

Monica. Her long hair fell free against her back. Her skin seemed luminous in the moon's light. She paused at the edge of the pier, knelt, and stared down at the water. Her hands dipped in and came back cupped with water. She held it up to her face, then let it slither through her fingers, trailing in silver rivulets down her wrists and forearms.

Without warning, she pivoted and looked up at him. Their eyes met. He quickly turned away.

4

PAUL GAZED DOWN at the opaque green water swelling against the boat's side. He shivered in the sharp morning chill. He wished he'd brought a sweater. Tendrils of mist swirled around them like miniature tornadoes, and overhead, a pale sun was waiting to burn through.

The water was strewn with debris, but Monica nosed the boat expertly around jagged timbers, car tires, plastic canisters, oil-slicked wooden spools.

He'd slept poorly—like some machine that wouldn't shut itself off—and this morning his body ached, and the inside of his mouth felt like cheap carpeting. He found himself sneaking glances at Monica's face. In the diffuse white light of the mist, she didn't look as pale as she had last night on the pier. He felt like a voyeur, peeping through windows, hoping for a bit of excitement. He should mind his own business.

"So why'd he run away?" she asked, her eyes fixed on the water.

Paul hesitated, then said, "Things weren't good for him at home."

That much was true. Sam had been so eager to get away from Governor's Hill, from Mom and Dad. From him. It was a kind of running away.

"He skipped a lot of grades at school. He didn't have many friends. He was way smarter than anyone his age but too small to mix with the older kids. He was always getting beaten up."

"So you were the bodyguard."

Paul nodded slowly, pleased. "I was always running interference for him on the way back and forth from school. Couldn't be with him all the time, though." He paused, uncomfortable. "A lot of it was his fault. He was lippy, pissing everyone off. If he'd have shut up, it would have been better for him."

"It must have been a pain, babysitting."

"It wasn't babysitting," he snapped angrily. But she was right; how many times had he used the same word himself?

Babysitting. It was a complicated feeling. He'd always felt like Sam's protector. Sometimes he'd have been happy to let him fend for himself. But whenever he thought of that one time, his throat contracted. They'd made him watch. No. He'd be seeing Sam soon, and everything would be all right.

Dark shapes loomed, then broke through the mist, a long line of decaying boathouses, some half submerged.

"That's the one," said Monica, pointing.

"How many times did you see him around here?"

"A couple," she answered.

"What was he doing?"

"Looking around. That's how I knew he was a stranger. It was funny, because at first. . ." She trailed off.

"What?"

"Nothing. You sure don't look like your brother."

"You never talked to him?"

"Why would I?"

She maneuvered slowly through the tangle of broken jetties. The outer doors of the boathouse were wide open, and she pushed the gears into neutral and swung inside. At the back, a set of stairs led up to a loft, partially concealed behind a low wall.

Monica nudged against the deck, looping the

painter deftly around a rusted metal cleat.

Paul was over the side at once.

"Sam!"

No answer.

"You sure this was the place?" he asked.

"This is it. Watch the planking. It looks rotten."

"Sam!"

He climbed up to the loft.

It was the disorder that sent the first shriek of alarm through his head. Clothes were scattered about, jeans, shirts, socks, underwear—he even recognized one of the T-shirts he'd given Sam on his last birthday. Sam never left anything lying around.

Paul's eyes picked out the broken remains of laboratory glassware. Several metal racks and some small lab implements were strewn nearby. Surely he'd brought more equipment than this! Where was it? And what about a sleeping bag? Food? He'd been down here for weeks. What was he living off?

"Looks like he cleared out," Monica said behind him.

But then he saw his brother's glasses, lying on the floor. Sam was almost blind without them. He'd never leave them behind.

There were endless possibilities here. You could slip from a pier, dash your head to pieces on the timbers below. You could drown, get mugged, murdered for an empty wallet. But none of these things explained the glasses. Sam would have been wearing them. Broken equipment, clothes all over. Signs of a struggle? Maybe. With whom? Sam, what happened here?

"Maybe he's planning on coming back."

Paul slipped the glasses into his pocket.

"No. He's not coming back."

What was Sam doing down here, holed up in a deserted boathouse with test tubes and beakers, like some kid on a demented school field trip? Maybe if he'd come right after Sam's phone call, instead of waiting a few days. Maybe it would have made a difference, maybe, maybe. He took a deep breath. There was nothing else to see here.

He gathered up the clothes. They still smelled of Sam. He brushed past Monica and headed down the steps, numb.

"We should have come last night," he muttered, knowing it was unfair.

"You saw what the waters are like around here," she said dispassionately.

"Something's happened to him!" he shouted. "He could be dead! And you didn't want to scratch your crappy boat!"

"Paul, I'm sorry! But it's not my problem!"

"Not your problem! That's great, that's just—"

He hit the last step and felt it give way. The crack of splintering wood sounded in his ears as he lurched headlong toward the water, the bundle of clothes spilling out ahead of him. Suddenly Monica's hand closed around his right arm, snapping him back. He was less surprised by the strength of her grip than by its coldness— an uncanny chill through the fabric of his sweatshirt.

He toppled clumsily to the deck, wrenching his foot free from the rotted wood. Sam's clothing floated atop the filthy water, already sodden. He started snatching it out with furious determination, slapping it against the deck. He hardened his face, biting back tears.

Monica knelt beside him and fished out a few T-shirts and socks. Paul couldn't look at her. He felt like a fool. He was captain of the track team, he could bench-press his own weight and more, and here he was, tripping on steps. She'd had to pull him back like a mother grabbing a little kid who'd wandered too close to the deep end! It wasn't his fault. This whole stinking place was rotting under his feet.

They carried the clothes back to the boat in silence.

"Thanks," he said grudgingly. "I'm sorry."

"You missed something up in the loft."

"What?"

She handed him a small square of plastic. It was a computer diskette. He blew off the dust and examined the label: S. B. Sam.

"Where was it?"

"Jammed against the wall."

The motor shuddered to life. Her pale hands tapped the steering wheel as she stared straight ahead. "Look, I hope you find your brother, really I do. Where do you want to go? I'll dump you anywhere you want."

Paul was still looking at the diskette. "Do you have a computer?"

"Paul, this is really none of my business." She hesitated, then said evenly, "What I mean is, I don't want to do this anymore."

He couldn't blame her. He was a total stranger and she'd already done a lot. He rubbed his arm. It was sore where she'd grabbed him.

"Yeah, I'm sorry," he said. "I really appreciate everything you've done."

She shrugged, avoiding his eyes. "Where do you want to go?"

"Can you take me back to the main pier?"

"Done. Get in." She started backing the boat out but then flipped it into neutral. "What are you going to do at the main pier?"

"I'll try to get a computer." He had no idea how.

"I can't stand people like you, Paul," she muttered. "I really can't. You are so damn helpless. How is someone like you going to get a line on a computer in Watertown? Yellow Pages?" She gave a snort of irritation. "I can't stand it. Ask Armitage about the computer when we get back. Maybe he's got something kicking around. If not, I want you out of my life for good."

Paul couldn't help smiling in relief.

"And I don't want another one of your suburban thank-yous."

The last of the morning fog was burning off. Monica reached for a pair of sunglasses and perched on the back of her seat for a better view of the debris-strewn water. Paul turned the diskette over and over in his hands, as if it would suddenly offer up secrets. It might give him an idea of what Sam was doing down here, what had happened to him.

"Bad news."

"What?" He scanned the water for menacing debris.

"Listen."

Paul heard nothing but the growl of their engine. Monica pulled the boat around in a sharp turn and opened up the throttle.

"What's going on?" Paul asked uneasily.

It was a few seconds before the rhythmic

thumping of rotor blades reached his ears. Then the helicopter broke through the veil of mist and drifted lazily over the boathouse roofs, in their direction.

A piece of debris knocked against the boat's hull, then deflected off the propeller with a sharp grinding noise. Monica swore but didn't slow down. But the helicopter had overtaken them, hovering low, shattering the water's surface. Paul clamped his hands over his ears, wincing.

"Who are they?" he shouted.

"Don't know," she yelled back. "But I don't think they're tourists."

With a sudden burst of speed, Monica aimed the boat straight at a high pier.

"Hey, what are you doing!" he shouted in alarm.

She hunched tighter over the wheel. Paul's fingers dug into the plastic upholstery of his seat. The boat veered crazily around pilings and timbers and then shot underneath the pier and into shadow, with about two feet of clearance overhead. The boat slowed to a gentle glide.

"How did you know we'd fit?" Paul asked weakly.

"I've done it before. If there's one thing I hate," Monica muttered, steering the boat carefully between the pilings, "it's unmarked helicopters."

"I think I saw that one yesterday."

"Me, too."

"It took a good long look at me."

She glanced over at him. "Armitage is not going to be happy."

"It's probably just some cops on their lunch break," said Armitage easily. "I wouldn't worry about it."

He was sitting cross-legged in the boathouse, a laser disc player in his skinny lap, a metal file in one hand. He paused to study his handiwork.

"What do you think?" he asked Paul. "Can you read that?"

Paul obligingly peered at a metal plate on the back of the machine. The serial number was completely filed away.

"Looks good to me."

"Take it from the expert," said Monica with soft sarcasm. Paul felt his face flush. The closest he got to the world of crime in Governor's Hill was the movies.

Armitage waved his file at the diskette in Paul's hand. "Runaways don't usually drag around portable computers."

"Sam's a strange guy," Paul replied awkwardly, hoping Armitage wouldn't pursue it.

Armitage replaced the laser disc player in its

box and stood up, dusting metal filings from his trousers.

"I don't have anything here right now," he said. "Tell you what, though, I've got to go into the docklands today for business. Why don't you let me take it in? I can get a hard copy run off for you."

Paul desperately wanted the magnetic secrets, but he knew he couldn't give the diskette to Armitage. *Tell no one*: Sam's words.

"I'd rather keep hold of it," Paul said. "If you don't mind."

Armitage looked at him for a long time.

"You don't trust me, Paul?"

Paul shuffled his feet awkwardly. "It's just that—"

"You're smart," Armitage said. "It's safer not to trust people. But I'm a busy man, Paul. You can't really expect me to bring back a computer, just for you."

"No." He'd overstepped again. "If you can't do it, you can't do it."

"I didn't say I can't do it. The question is, Will I do it? I can get anything I want out there."

"I'm sure you can," Paul said quickly; he didn't want any raised hackles.

"You don't believe me?"

"I do. Really." He didn't want a scene.

"I can get anything I want out of this town. I'll get your computer. I'm going to further your education, Paul. You can do a project on it when you get back to school—something on bristol board maybe. But it might take a day or two."

Paul couldn't help smiling. "Um, all right."

But Monica was shaking her head angrily. "Forget it, Armitage. It's time for him to go."

"What are you talking about?" asked Armitage.

"I've got a bad feeling about this. There was an unmarked helicopter out there. He said it spooked him yesterday as he was coming here. And there it was again when we were leaving the boathouse. Am I the only person who sees a connection? For all we know, this brother of his could be wanted by the cops."

"He's not—" Paul began to protest.

"They got a good look at me, Armitage, and I don't like that. You shouldn't either. If they trace him here, we go down."

"Paranoid," her brother said dismissively.

"What the hell's wrong with you?" she demanded.

"They were probably just standard pass-overs."

"You're getting careless."

"I'm not getting careless. I know exactly what

I'm doing! I'm staying real sharp. All you have to do is go through people's pockets, okay? The rest is for me to worry about!"

"What about your rule? No strangers on the pier."

"You brought him, Monica."

"For one night. I felt sorry for him, okay? And now I'm getting edgy."

Paul could only watch, mortified. He'd grown up with tense silences, unspoken words, dark looks at the dinner table. People weren't supposed to fight like this, especially not in public. People were supposed to keep it in.

"You're talking crap!" Armitage said. "I haven't screwed up yet. I'm holding things together for us—better than Mom ever did."

"Shut up, Armitage!"

"Mom's not here anymore! Good thing, too, 'cause she was useless!"

"She taught you," Monica said coldly. "Stealing—and lots of other things, too."

"Yeah, she did. And then she let it all fall apart!"

Monica seemed to lose all her fire. She shrugged indifferently. "So you want me to stick around here all day, that it?"

"I wanted you to have a look at the cabin cruiser, anyway," said Armitage. "The engine's been acting up, and you know it better than anyone else. Work some magic with it, okay?"

It was a kind of peace offering, but Monica didn't seem particularly pleased. "Fine, but I'm not going to babysit the boy genius."

"I don't need a babysitter," Paul said quietly.

Monica shook her head wearily. "You sure as hell do. I'm just sorry we don't have any board games."

"Have you finished?" Paul asked.

"Not yet."

Board games were a passion with Sam. The most complicated ones, war games, with rule books as thick as school texts, boards that folded out over half the living room floor, and hundreds of tiny cardboard counters with symbols and numbers in every corner.

"You said you wouldn't take so long this time."

"I'm almost done."

Paul rolled his eyes. Sam seemed to spend an eternity analyzing every possibility. Paul didn't have the patience for games that dragged on all afternoon and sometimes longer. He couldn't take it all that seriously. Besides, he always got decimated.

"Ready," Sam proclaimed.

"Let's hear it, General," said Paul sarcastically.

Sam read out his orders, expertly annihilating Paul's best tanks and artillery. Paul shook his head, dazed. Sam always seemed to be three or four moves ahead of him. Paul didn't stand a chance. He reluctantly read out his orders and actually fired mistakenly on his own troops.

"This is boring," he said.

"It's just getting good," Sam said distractedly, already studying the board for his next set of victorious moves.

"Boring," Paul said again.

"You're not concentrating," Sam scolded him. "Honestly, Paul, you have to think it through."

"Let's go outside."

Sam sighed. "You're just angry because you're losing."

"I'm not angry. I'm just bored! Come on. We can call David and Barry and get a game of touch football going."

He knew Sam hated playing games outside, but he wanted to go to the park, get his body into the sun, stretch his muscles.

"No thanks," said his brother in a tight voice. "All you want to do is sit on your ass reading books or playing these games."

"The doctor said I shouldn't overexert myself."

Sam's doctors—the names changed every few months or so, as his parents became dissatisfied

46

with the treatment. His brother would come back from his appointments with more pills, more instructions. And the fact was, he hadn't put on a single pound in months. Paul knew he was supposed to be understanding, but he spent enough time playing bodyguard at school. Was he really expected to stay indoors on weekends and let Sam pulverize him with his war games?

"Maybe if you got more exercise—" he began testily.

"Playing football with your half-wit friends is not the solution."

"Don't be such a wimp!"

"Look, you always want to stop in the middle of the games. Grow up. If you put in more of an effort, there's a small chance you'd make fewer moronic mistakes!"

Paul swiped his hand across the playing board, knocking all the counters onto the carpet.

"That was stupid!" shouted Sam.

"This game is stupid."

"There's more to life than track meets and bodybuilding, Paul."

Before Paul could stop himself, he shoved Sam sprawling against the sofa. He'd never hit him before.

"Don't call me stupid," he muttered halfheartedly, startled by the rage in his brother's face.

"Don't ever do that again!" Sam's voice crackled. "You can't treat me like that! You're nothing without me!"

Paul only stared numbly, knowing that Sam was right.

5

SHE WAS WORKING in the engine hatch of the cabin cruiser, so Paul could see only her hunched head and shoulders above the deck. Occasionally, a grease-smudged hand darted out for the tools arranged nearby. He listened to the efficient sounds of metal on metal and felt inadequate.

"Can I help?"

She glanced up, wisps of dark hair hanging untidily around her face. She pushed them away, leaving a streak of soot across her cheekbone.

"I don't know. Can you?"

Her ferocity startled him. He jammed his hands into his pockets. "No." He didn't know anything about boats or motors.

"Why'd you ask then?"

She disappeared beneath the hatch.

"I'm sorry about earlier," he said awkwardly. "I didn't mean to start a fight between you and Armitage."

"Forget it," came her muffled voice. "Happens all the time. Armitage doesn't like it when you criticize his little empire."

"Empire?"

She lifted her face to him. "Come on, Paul, haven't you got us pigeonholed by now?"

His eyes roved across the neat stacks of cardboard boxes against the walls. He couldn't help his automatic reaction. It was wrong to steal.

"Armitage is a businessman," she said from below. "It's the truth, more or less. Everyone on our pier works for him—including me, I suppose. Whatever we take in, Armitage sinks into merchandise. He buys it right off the freighters, cheap. The freight handlers adjust their inventories. Armitage files off serial numbers and resells the goods in the City for big profits. He's doing well." She laughed softly. "He's even got his own bank account in the City—under a fake name, of course. He's a good old-fashioned entrepreneur. Pass me the vise grips."

He was pleased to have been given a job. He looked at the tools and took a guess.

"Paul, these are needlenose pliers." She reappeared from the engine hatch. "Tell me, do you have any skills, besides being a bodyguard?"

She said it jokingly, but he was taken aback. He felt an absurd urge to launch into a list of the track ribbons he'd won, how much he could curl, his lap times in the pool. And maybe his school marks, too—they weren't so bad.

Monica grunted and grabbed the vise grips. "Armitage wants to rebuild this place. He hates it that everyone in the City thinks Watertown's a slum. So he wants to make a lot of money and change things here." She added dubiously, "That's his plan, anyway."

"You don't think it'll work?"

"Oh, it might," she replied, ducking down again. "Just don't know if I like the idea. There's good things about it, I suppose. Armitage's little bank account paid for our water tower on the pier, the big gate to keep people out, electric generators, the boats. We live pretty well. Seems to me, though, that if it goes too far, we won't be an island anymore. It'll turn into—I don't know—just another suburb. We'll get people like you showing up all the time, making rules, screwing everything up."

"Don't worry, I'm not here to stay," said Paul, surprised that her words had stung him.

"Well," she said, "you're sure stirring things up."

"Not enough, obviously."

Armitage had left for the docklands almost two hours ago but might not be back for a couple of days. What was he supposed to do in the meantime? Where was Sam now; what was he doing? He paced restlessly, tormented by the thought of all the wasted time. There must be something he could do.

"I've been thinking about the police," he began carefully.

"It's too risky." Monica gestured around the boathouse. "What would they think of all this, huh? One look, and me and Armitage get sent to some group detention home in the suburbs. No way."

"They wouldn't have to know about you or Armitage."

She slammed down the vise grips and hoisted herself up onto the deck.

"Fine," he said. "No police. I'm just trying to find my brother."

"You two must be close," she said. He thought there was a trace of wistfulness in her voice.

Paul felt an unexpected fluttering of arousal. He didn't know why. She was too thin, too pointy, and she was probably flat, though it was impossible to tell through all the layers of clothing. The girls he liked in Governor's Hill were curvier, healthy looking, with tans they managed to hold on to year-round. His eyes traveled over the sharp angles of Monica's pale face, her mop of uncontrollable hair. She was like no girl he'd ever seen.

"I suppose we were—we are, yes." Lately he'd caught himself thinking about Sam in the past tense. It had been months since they'd last seen each other, and they hadn't parted on the best of terms. A silent, awkward handshake.

"You came all the way down here to look for him," she said. "Sounds like you take pretty good care of him."

Paul felt the familiar spasm of guilt—the circle of jeering faces, Sam on the ground, Randy Smith astride him. Paul watched, helpless. There was nothing he could do. They held him back.

"So how does he pay you back for all your bodyguard services?"

"What do you mean?" Paul asked nervously.

"He must help you with your homework, right?"

"Sometimes, sure," he answered, relieved.

"Come on, Paul, you know what I mean," she said quietly. "Didn't he ever tell you you were really stupid?" There was an almost vindictive quality in her voice.

"Sometimes he wasn't as patient as he—"

"You were doing your two-times tables and he was doing E equals mc squared, right? And he didn't make you feel like a total moron? He never rubbed it in? You with all the nice big muscles?"

"That's enough." His heart was pounding, and a sweaty prickle was working its way down his back.

"You must have been real pissed off—all those put-downs."

"Sometimes, maybe," he stammered. "It wasn't so bad."

"You beat him up, didn't you?"

"I did not beat him up!"

"That's why he ran away."

"You don't know what you're talking about! They beat him up, not me! I was the one who stopped them!" He jabbed a thumb defiantly toward his chest. "I was the one who protected him all the time. Me. And he just took it for granted. He didn't even notice the things I did for him!"

He'd run out of breath, and all at once felt horribly empty. Maybe he'd just needed to spit out the words, like the crazy lady on the main pier, shouting her litany of persecution to anyone who passed.

"That wasn't fair, what I just said," he told her anxiously. "He had a lot to put up with, too. More than me. I mean, I didn't get what he got. It could have been me, but it was Sam."

"I'm sorry," said Monica.

"Why did you do that? Say those things?"

"I just wanted to know what made him leave. It was stupid of me."

He shrugged, feeling a little sick.

"How do you know he's even in Watertown? Maybe he just packed up, went home."

"He's blind without his glasses."

And Sam would never return to Governor's Hill. Neither of those things necessarily meant that Sam was still here in Watertown. But there was something else—that shadowy figure dancing across the rooftops. Why that electric jolt of recognition? All he'd seen was a knife-edged silhouette—no face, no details. Sam couldn't run that fast, and he certainly couldn't make those jumps.

"What's the place we met at?" he asked with sudden urgency.

"Jailer's Pier."

"No, I mean the place on the other side."

She seemed hesitant. "It's where the old prisons used to be."

"There was a jail here?" he asked, surprised.

"This whole place was a jail once. I guess they don't teach that up in Governor's Hill."

"No."

"It goes back more than two hundred years. The City prisons were overcrowded, so someone came up with the idea of putting convicts out in the harbor. They tethered a couple old hulks together and made a prison island."

He followed her along the pier and up the ladder into the stilt house.

"So, you stole a loaf of bread, you were sent to the hulks," she said. "Below deck you couldn't even stand upright. Tiny, cramped spaces, bodies pressing against you all the time. Epidemics wiped out whole ships. Prisoners sometimes tried to swim back to shore. Not many made it—they had these iron balls chained around their wrists and ankles."

"When did they shut it down?"

"About a hundred and fifty years ago. The ships were taking on too much water. But some of the convicts stayed. Wasn't long before most of the hulks rotted away completely, but the piers and jetties were still there. Over the years, more and more people came."

"How did you learn all this?"

"My mom told me."

"So, across the canal, that was where the last hulks were anchored?"

She nodded. "Watertowners call it Rat Castle."

"Why don't people live there anymore?"

"They're stupid. Superstitious."

"Ghosts?"

"I guess," she said.

"But someone could be hiding in there."

"There's no one there, Paul."

"But how can you be certain?"

"You think because you saw something it means your brother's in there? I've seen things, too." She lifted her hands in a gesture of futility. "People disappear here all the time."

"Your parents."

His words startled him.

"I never knew my father." She shrugged. "He did the vanishing act before I was born. Armitage might remember him, but I doubt it."

"What about your mother?"

"She went eight months ago."

"How?" he asked awkwardly. "Did she die?"

"She walked out. Another runaway."

She spoke with complete indifference. He felt a pang of tenderness for her, but there was a spark of excitement, too. They had something in common.

"Maybe she'll come back."

"I'm not holding my breath. Anyway, Armitage is right. She was useless. We're better off without her."

"Oh."

"She used to be a teacher at some college before she ended up down here. She taught history. One day she couldn't stand it anymore. She said there was no point because it just didn't get any better. The tyranny of the past. Anyway, she just shredded all her work and went wandering. I guess that's what you call a nervous breakdown."

Paul waited, not wanting to break the mood.

"Armitage and I were born here. She brought us up, but she just wasn't all there. She'd go off every now and then. One day she didn't come back. End of story."

"But you still look for her, don't you?"

"Not much point, really."

"You look for her by Rat Castle."

She didn't answer for a few seconds. "She used to wander around there sometimes, that's all. I found her on Jailer's Pier once or twice. Looking at the water."

Paul thought of her last night, cupping the water in her hands, letting it slither through her fingers.

"So, what about the rest of your family?" she asked quickly. "What are your parents like?"

With a start he realized how little he thought about them; they were so distant from his everyday life. Usually they were both gone when he got up in the morning, and they didn't come home from work until seven. Work—that was it, he could start with that.

"Well," he began, "my mom is an insurance adjuster."

Monica's nose wrinkled. "What's that?"

"I don't know." And he laughed with her. "I swear, I have no idea what that means!"

"What about your dad?"

"He's a sales rep for a company that makes, um, business forms."

"Oh, a stiff."

"A what?"

"You know, like a corpse—because his job's so boring."

Paul grinned. "I guess."

"But what are they like? Do you like them?"

If she had asked whether he loved them, he could have automatically answered yes. But did he like them? That was different.

"I . . . I guess I don't know them," he said, a little bewildered.

"Well, you never do, do you?" she said matter-of-factly. "Anyone in your family. I don't think I know Armitage very well." She paused, looking at him carefully. "And how well do you know Sam?"

He held the pose in front of the mirror, chest heaving from the push-ups. He studied his reflection critically, forcing himself to hold the position even though it was beginning to hurt. When he was younger, he'd been afraid that one day he'd wake up to find himself like Sam—losing weight, shriveling up. It still lingered, that irrational fear, always at the back of his mind as he pushed and strained against the gym machines.

But there was another reason he'd worked so slavishly for his body. He liked the strength. It gave him power. Power over Sam. Sam needed his muscles.

"So you've got one wish," Sam said. "What do you do with it?"

It was a game they often played.

"Just one wish?" Paul asked.

"This time, just one," he said, setting down his notebook.

"Can I ask for more wishes, as my wish?"

"Sorry."

Sam wasn't normally so stingy with the wishes. Three was the usual number—it gave you some room to play around, to find out what you really wanted. Sometimes the games were serious, but mostly their wishes became more and more ridiculous until they were shrieking with laughter.

When he was younger, Paul almost always

wished for things: video games, a portable stereo, new track shoes. Occasionally, he wished his parents wouldn't fight so much or that Sam's new pills would work. Lately he'd been wishing for various girls in his class, a better lap time on his fifty-meter crawl, a fraction of an inch on the high jump.

Just one wish. It was a serious game. What did he want? It had been on his mind quite a lot recently. He didn't want to be separated from his brother.

Sam had just applied for early admission to college. If he got in, he'd be leaving home next fall. The two of them had often talked about leaving Governor's Hill together, being roommates. It was silly, he supposed, because he lagged years behind Sam at school. But they'd still talked about it, made plans, imagined what it would be like to live in a new place. Their rules only.

Sam had seemed so eager when he'd filled out his applications, as if he'd forgotten about their plans. Or maybe they just didn't matter. Hadn't Sam known how hurt Paul would be if he went away to college?

"My wish," he said, losing courage, "is for a shower with Susan White."

"That's it?" said Sam.

"Yeah. What about yours?"

"Forget it."

"Why?"

"You're not taking this seriously."

"I just couldn't think, that's all. Tell me your wish anyway."

Sam wouldn't look up at him. He was sketching in his notebook, tracing lines, shading in with the side of his pencil.

"At the doctor's this afternoon," he said in a conversational tone, "he left the room for a few minutes. My file was just lying there on his desk. You should see the size of it!" He spread two of his fingers, grinning, and Paul found himself grinning back uneasily.

"I couldn't resist. I wanted to see all this stuff about me—charts, letters, ECG scrolls, X-ray results. You thought my textbooks were bad!"

Paul chuckled nervously.

"I was looking at this one lab report, and my eyes caught the words 'Life Expectancy.' So I kept reading."

Paul's smile congealed on his face. "What did it say?"

"I've got a best-before date. Between twenty-three and twenty-seven years old."

"You're joking, right?"

"No."

"Mom and Dad never said anything!"

"They got a letter," Sam said. "A copy of it was in the file, too. Obviously they didn't want me to know."

"Maybe it's a mistake," said Paul. "Some of your other tests were wrong. They can't know stuff like that!"

He wanted to hug his brother—but something held him back. They didn't ever really hug, but it was more than that. He felt a vague sense of revulsion, of anger. Sam was letting this happen to him! He could fight back if he wanted!

His gaze suddenly dropped down to Sam's open notebook. On the front page was a sketch of da Vinci's perfect man, but half the body was mechanical metal limbs, rubber arteries, a chrome rib cage, and a stainless-steel heart.

"So my wish," said Sam, "is to heal myself."

"Sam!"

He woke with a shudder, still half convinced that his brother had been standing over him, watching as he slept. Wimp, he told himself. But an electric buzz seemed to linger in the air.

He stood and looked out over the pier. At first he thought it was Monica again, standing in shadow at the water's edge. But when the figure shifted slightly, Paul knew it wasn't her. He whispered his brother's name through his dry mouth, but the figure darted across the pier so quickly he lost sight of it. He rushed out and onto the outer steps. Shivering in the cool of the night, he scanned the pier, and when he saw nothing, he dashed up to the roof for a better view.

"Shhhh!" A cold hand closed around his forearm. Monica moved up beside him. "I saw it, too," she whispered. "There." She pointed down to the end of the pier, near the high iron gate. "See?"

"No," Paul told her. "You must have damn good eyesight. Who is it?"

"Can't tell."

The figure leaped and cleared the gate, disappearing into the maze of alleyways on the other side. Gooseflesh broke out over Paul's arms and legs.

"That gate must be over ten feet high!"

"Twelve and a half."

"Have you ever seen anything like that before?"

She seemed to hesitate, then shook her head. "You think it's your brother, don't you?"

"Maybe," he replied guardedly.

She rubbed sleep from her eyes. She'd dressed quickly, in only a single sweatshirt and trousers. She was very tiny. Paul was suddenly aware that he wore nothing but his underpants.

He half turned away from her, his arms automatically folding across his chest, as if trying to conceal as much of his body as possible. But when he realized she wasn't taking the slightest notice of him, he felt slightly put out, then ridiculous.

"We could ask Decks tomorrow," she said. "He used to work on a tug in the harbor. He's been around Watertown for ages. He might have seen your brother."

"Thanks," he said gratefully, trying to stand up straight.

"Get some sleep, Muscles."

6

"**Y**OU AREN'T THE first person to ask me about this boy." Decks handed the photograph back to Paul. "Two men came around over a week ago with a picture and asked if I'd seen him. I told them no, which is what I would have told any stranger spooking for somebody. In this case, it's also the truth. I haven't seen him."

Paul's heart raced. He glanced at Monica, sitting across from him in the narrow galley of Decks's houseboat.

"Cops," she said tersely. "I knew it. Those damn helicopters. Why would the police be looking for your brother, Paul? Who sent them? Your parents?"

"They don't know he's down here." Unless

they had somehow found out. Had the university gotten in touch with them? But Sam said he'd quit his research job, so the university wouldn't have known where he was either.

"I don't think it was the police," said Decks, scratching at the stubble on his chin. He had broad, heavily callused hands and a gruff voice that made Paul feel small and uncertain.

"The police don't come down here for runaways or missing persons. Watertown's like a maze to them. These two weren't wearing uniforms, didn't show any identification. Whoever they are, they didn't come because someone's parents called. They had holsters under their jackets."

Monica's gaze settled hard on Paul. "Your brother's not really a runaway, is he?"

It was pointless to try to hide it now. Armed men—looking for Sam.

"He was doing research for the university, studying samples from the dead water zone. He told me he'd found something strange, something he didn't understand. No one knew he was coming down, and he asked me not to tell anyone either."

He saw Monica's eyes flicker over to Decks.

"Why didn't you tell us that right away?" she demanded.

"I didn't think it was important."

"You lied to me, Paul."

He thought he caught a look of genuine hurt in her face, but it was quickly blocked out by anger.

"What about all that other stuff you told me yesterday, huh? About you and your brother. Was all that bullshit, too?"

"No."

"Just thought you could use us, right?"

"I promised him," he blurted.

"I should make you swim back to shore. You had no idea your brother was being hunted?"

Hunted. The loft at the old boathouse. A pile of clothes, glasses in the dust, shattered glassware, a dropped diskette. Maybe they'd surprised him; maybe he was asleep when they came. Paul played it out in his mind: they had crept noiselessly up the stairs, Sam not even waking until they'd seized him, his shouts muffled by a hand clamped across his mouth. He hadn't even had time to grab for his glasses.

"Maybe they're ahead of me," he said, sick. "Maybe they found him at the boathouse."

"I don't think so," said Monica. "Why would that helicopter tail us afterward? They must have thought one of us was Sam."

Decks nodded in agreement. "I saw a helicopter making passes late yesterday afternoon. If they'd found your brother, they'd be long gone by now."

"He might have known they were looking for him and left on his own," said Paul, hopeful.

Another reassuring thought came to mind— the shadowy figure on the pier last night. There was no logical proof it had been Sam, but it somehow gave him hope.

"Must have been pretty heavy-duty research," said Monica. "And he didn't say anything else about it?"

"Nothing."

"Why'd you come down here, then? Unless you knew he was in trouble?"

"It was just a feeling."

She wouldn't believe him, even though this part was true. Last night, on the rooftop, he had felt almost close to her, but now . . . "When we last talked on the phone, he sounded funny. He was really worked up. I think he was scared, too. I was worried."

"Very helpful," she said witheringly. She turned to Decks. "There's a computer diskette, too. I found it in the boathouse. Armitage is trying to get a machine so we can read it."

Paul's hand involuntarily touched the diskette in his shirt pocket. "It might be a jumble to anyone but Sam. But there could be a clue to where he is."

"And what he's been doing," Monica added. "I think you're holding out on us, Paul."

"I've told you everything." There was more, but it was strictly personal. Sometimes he barely understood it himself.

"This is getting very messy," said Monica. "If they trace us back to our pier—"

Paul felt an urge to reach across and brush away the purple smudges of fatigue beneath her eyes.

"Look," he said apologetically, "I wasn't trying to make trouble. I came down here to meet my brother. He told me to come to Jailer's Pier. He didn't show up."

"That's where I found him," Monica told Decks. "Now he's got it into his head that his brother might be hiding out in Rat Castle. What do you think?"

Decks snorted. "The canal runs all the way around, like a moat. Anyway, the whole place was boarded up years ago. All the piers were rotting away."

"See?" she said, but Paul thought there was vague disappointment on her face, too.

"You should stay away from there," Decks told Monica. "It's not safe. It won't be long before it collapses to the bottom of the lake."

"Thanks, Decks," said Monica. "You've been a help."

At the hatchway, Decks placed a hand on Paul's arm. "There's one other thing I should tell you," he said. "That photograph they showed me—you were in it, too."

"When we get back to the pier, you're staying inside. Understand?"

Paul nodded mutely, keeping pace with her through the maze of alleyways. His mind kept circling back to the photograph of him and Sam. When had it been taken? Where? What were he and Sam doing? The details seemed important somehow. Get a grip, he told himself. But how had they got hold of it? He imagined them going through the closets of his brother's room at college, handling his clothes, pulling pictures from the bulletin board. Paul suddenly felt afraid.

"Runaway brother," Monica was muttering. "What crap!"

"Why are they carrying guns?" he said. "What's the point of guns?"

"You tell me. Maybe they want something your brother has."

"What do you know about the water?"

"What are you talking about?" She looked at him, surprised.

"It's got to have something to do with the water. He said there was something strange about it."

"It's polluted. Nothing lives in it. You can't drink it."

"He found something new. He didn't say what."

"What was it about the water?" she asked fiercely. "What are you so afraid of?"

"That he'll kill himself."

He was almost as surprised as she was.

"What?"

He shook his head. "It was a stupid thing to say."

"Why would he do that? Because he got beat up at school?"

Paul didn't have time to answer. Three kids slid out from an alcove on the jetty, mean looking, all wearing ripped-to-hell black jeans, shredded at the seams and held together with safety pins and staples. Torn shirts hung down past worn-out jackets; metal-toed boots sounded against the planking. He felt his jaw tense, sweat prickle under his arms. Monica touched his hand lightly. *Let me handle this.*

With predictability that almost made him laugh, the three kids languidly blocked their way. It was strangely familiar—kids gathered on a school playground. Bullies everywhere. In Governor's Hill he was used to shouted threats, intimidation, ridicule, maybe a few hard shoves.

But a part of him exulted. He was bigger than any of them, but the numbers weren't fair. Out of the corner of his eye he admired the vaguely bored look on Monica's face.

The kid in front had long, dirty dreadlocks. His face and neck were tattooed with cobwebs and spiders. Four metal loops were sunk through one of his nostrils, and a safety pin had been plunged through the inflamed flesh at the bridge of his nose.

"Wanderin' around as if she owns the place."

"Don't you have anything better to do than piss me off, Sked?" Monica replied.

"Well, this is interesting." Sked turned his dark gaze on Paul. "A City boy."

"Move it," said Monica. "This is boring."

"Does your City friend here know you're a health hazard, Toxic Freak?"

Paul felt a nervous tremor working its way through his body. "Get out of the way," he said.

Sked slammed a thick hand onto his arm. Paul found himself staring at the kid's knuckles, the flesh torn away in ragged patches.

"Seen your brother lately?"

Paul wrenched his arm free, fury gathering like a white-hot burn in the center of his chest. "What do you know about my brother?" he said, choking on his words. If these bastards had Sam . . .

"We're just asking if you've seen him lately."

"Where is he?" Paul shouted. His ears roared with white noise. He was watching them all at once. They were moving in tighter.

"You know where he is, City boy. So just tell us. Save yourself a beating."

"Go to hell."

"Look at all this money they gave you, Sked," said Monica, waving a wad of bills. "How much did those two goons pay you to find his brother? Half now, half later, was that the arrangement?" She hurled the crumpled bills contemptuously in the air.

It took Sked a second to realize it was his money fluttering down around him. "You stinking freak!" he spat, and his hand came up, palm flat, aimed at Monica's face.

"Hey!" Paul shouted.

But Monica had slipped to one side, her arm darting out so quickly that Paul heard the impact of her fist before he realized she'd struck. Sked's head snapped back, an almost comical look of surprise on his face.

"Don't do this, Sked," Monica warned him. "Remember last time?"

Sked lunged for her as the other two came crashing in on Paul. His fists flew out, driving them back. In his sudden explosion of adrenaline, he felt like a machine: steel tendons, spring-loaded muscles, iron limbs smashing forward like pistons.

He watched Monica weave around Sked, avoiding his outstretched hands. Paul tried to get over to her, but the boys were blocking his way. They surged forward together, grabbing hold of his shoulders, kicking at his kneecaps, and slammed him to the planking. He twisted over onto his side, legs instinctively pulled up.

"Where's your brother?" they shouted at him. "Where is he?"

For just an instant he was Sam, pinned on the ground, Randy Smith's spit smeared across his face. So this was what it was like. Not the pain but the humiliation.

He intercepted a boot aimed at his ribs, locking his hands around the ankle and pulling with all his weight. The kid kicked frantically, arms flailing for balance, and toppled. Paul scrambled to his feet. *Where's your brother? Where's your brother?* He took a punch in the face—no pain, only a moment of blackness, and he felt a wet trickle in his nose. He lashed out again, the staccato pounding of his heart in his ears. They couldn't do this to him. But they had him in a headlock, gasping for breath.

"Where's your brother, you rich City wimp?"

Through the tangle of limbs, Paul saw that Monica had Sked's arm pinned against his back in a painful hold.

"You want me to let go?" she panted in Sked's ear. "Tell your high-fashion friends to let him go, or I'll break it for you."

"Try it," Sked breathed, his face ashen. Monica adjusted her grip on Sked's arm and he suddenly winced. "Let him go!"

Paul shrugged his way out of the headlock and moved past the two spider boys warily. Still holding Sked's arm in a pincer grip, Monica followed after him along the jetty.

"Don't move," Monica called back to the two boys, "or you can figure out how to sew his arm back on."

They were clawing at Sked's cash, crushing it into their pockets. The jetty opened out on one side, revealing discolored water licking around the pilings. Monica brought Sked up short.

"Not much fun, was it?" she said.

"Yeah, sure, maybe if I had what you all had—"

"Shut up," Monica said sharply. "Tell us what you know."

"Up yours."

Monica encouraged him with a slight rotation of his arm.

"They asked me if I'd seen this kid, your brother." He jerked his head at Paul.

"When?" asked Paul.

"A while ago, I don't know. They show me a photo. You're in it, too. I go, No, I ain't seen him. But I might get around to it. How much is it worth to you? And he says, Lots. Do I look rich? I need that cash. So he gives me some. Tells me to find out where your brother is, fast, and I'd get twice as much again."

"Why are they looking for him?"

"You tell me!" Another grunt of pain. "They didn't say, right? They didn't tell me nothing else. I saw you, thought you'd know."

Paul noticed that Sked's two friends were edging forward along the jetty. "Let's go," he said.

"Yeah, why don't you," Sked snorted, twisting his head around to look at Monica. "You're running out of time. Freaks like you can't last forever, right?"

Monica gave him a shove that sent him over the edge of the jetty.

"Run!" she shouted.

Paul bolted after Monica, through the maze of floating alleys, ducking beneath lines of laundry, soaring over gaps in rotted planking. He was pushing to keep up; his lungs began burning. He was grateful when she began to slack off, glancing over her shoulder to make sure they'd lost Sked's friends. He staggered to a standstill, hands on hips, breathing hard.

"Your nose is still bleeding."

He grunted and pinched his nostrils. He could feel the bruises on his body. "Where'd you learn to fight like that?"

She shrugged. "Pretty standard stuff. It only works on Sked because he's so stupid."

"I don't get it. I mean, I'm getting the crap knocked out of me, and you just twist Sked's arm—game over!"

"Don't get so angry!"

"I'm not angry!"

"You're shouting."

He shook his head. He'd thought he could hold his own. His body was the one thing he had confidence in. It worked—it used to anyway. He looked at Monica critically. Under the layers of baggy clothing, there was almost nothing to her. It didn't seem possible that she could have so much strength or endurance.

"Anyone could do what I did," she said. "It's just a trick."

"Yeah?" His arm was still tender where she'd grabbed him the other day.

"You had two guys on you. They were big. Don't worry about it."

All he knew was that since he'd arrived, it was all he could do to avoid snapping ladders, breaking rotted planking, tripping into the water. She was always two steps ahead of him.

"Yeah, well," he said. "I don't like getting beat up."

She was smiling.

"What's so funny?"

"It's your nose. You sound like a hand puppet."

Mortified, he released the tight grip on his nostrils. Short of dressing up in a chicken suit, there weren't many ways left to humiliate himself.

"So, who were they?"

"The local punks."

"They sure seem to hate you."

"We've had a few run-ins before. They hate everyone on our pier. We're doing pretty well for ourselves—makes people jealous. Sked's half crazy anyway, all the glue he sniffs."

"Why was he saying those things about you?" *Toxic freak. Health hazard.* "What was that all about?"

"What kind of things did they say about your brother? People like Sked say anything if they think it'll cut you. But whoever paid them off is going to a lot of trouble to find your brother."

Suddenly her face blanched alarmingly, and

her whole body sagged slightly, as if something inside had collapsed.

"You all right?"

She leaned against him, just for a moment. She seemed to weigh nothing at all. He felt the chill of her body through the clothing.

"Just winded," she said. "Let's get back to the pier."

Paul walked carefully through the wreckage of the living room. The rugs and tapestries had been torn from the walls and ceilings, chairs overturned, a set of shelves toppled across the floor. He followed Monica as she slowly inspected the stilt house, pausing before doorways, letting her eyes travel over the smashed furniture, the debris on the floor.

"They really did a job on it," she said in a neutral voice.

"Sked must have told them."

"No, not enough time. No one could have done all this in fifteen minutes."

"Decks."

She shook her head as if in a daze.

"Why not? Maybe they paid him off, too, just like Sked. He could have called them. He had plenty of time!"

"Shut up," she said sharply. "Just shut up for a

second, would you! I've got to think!"

"They were obviously looking for something," Paul persisted, gesturing wildly around the ravaged room. He yanked the diskette from his pocket and shook it in the air. "And Decks was the only person we told about this!"

"They were in my house, Paul! Can you understand what that feels like?"

He was startled by the anguish in her eyes. This was his fault. "I'm sorry," he said lamely.

"Sorry is a very overrated word."

"I'll pay for it," he blurted. "I'll get everything fixed or replaced."

"Yeah, right," she scoffed. "Out of your allowance, or will Mom and Dad put a check in the mail?"

He had stooped over to right a set of shelves and was now picking things off the floor at random.

"We were broken into once, in Governor's Hill." He knew it was a ridiculous comparison, but he wanted to make her feel better, and it was all that came to mind. "You feel violated, dirty."

"Yeah," she said softly, "you do. Look, just don't touch anything, okay? Not right now." She took a deep breath.

"Decks didn't tip them off. He wouldn't do that. They must have been keeping an eye on us

81

all along—maybe even as far back as the boathouse. Must have known we had the diskette."

She snatched the diskette from Paul and waved it in front of his face. "What's on here, Paul?"

"I don't know."

"I should smash this thing!"

She made as if to crack the plastic casing, and Paul lunged forward to stop her. They tumbled to the floor, wrestling, and the diskette skittered across the planking. Paul pulled back from her, breathing hard. Her eyes shone with tears.

"Damn it," she said darkly, "you build a gate and you figure you can keep people out, keep them from screwing up your life! I made a promise after Mom disappeared. Everything under control. No craziness. Just perfect order."

Paul wanted to say he was sorry, wanted to repeat it a hundred times. But she was right: words wouldn't undo what had happened. He'd been so consumed with finding Sam that he hadn't given much thought to the risks she was taking for him. She kept her pain so hidden away—all that strength in such a frail-looking body.

She sat up. "Armitage is back."

Paul listened and a few moments later heard the motorboat pulling under the stilt house. He pushed the diskette back into his pocket. The door creaked as Armitage entered. Paul heard him swear softly under his breath before he came into view around the corner, a look of blank amazement on his face.

"It turns out there's some people looking for his brother," Monica said.

"Yeah," Armitage replied softly, "I know. I was picking up rumors all around the docklands. I think it's Cityweb."

"Who?" Paul asked, nervous.

"They don't have badges or uniforms; they don't even have names half the time. They do the stuff that even the police would rather not know about."

"Sked and some of his nice friends attacked us on the way back from Decks's place. They'd been paid off. Wanted to know where Paul's brother was."

"So," began Armitage, looking at Paul, "why all this special treatment for your brother?"

"He's not a runaway," Paul answered. "He came down here to do some tests on the dead water zone. He told me he'd found something weird."

Armitage looked at his sister for a long time before turning back to face Paul. "This is all you know, huh?"

"Yes."

"You stupid bastard!" Armitage exploded, grabbing him by the shirt. "Look at this place!"

"Leave him alone, Armitage," said Monica.

"Don't stick up for him!"

"'The helicopters aren't anything to worry about.' Who said that? Remind me! Who invited him to move in?"

"I didn't know about any of this other stuff!"

"Did you get the computer?" she asked.

Armitage looked at her in confusion. "In the boat, why?"

"Bring it up. Let's see what's on this diskette."

Paul thought the last thing she'd want to do was help him.

"Forget it," said Armitage. "We wash our hands right now."

"Come on, Armitage. They already know we're involved. Best thing we can do is find his brother and clear them both out of here."

"Maybe we should just hand over the diskette," Armitage suggested.

"What?" Paul was incredulous.

"It's like this, Paul. Some of my docklands partners are getting edgy—they think these Cityweb goons are trying to shut me down. I will not have someone screwing up my business, know what I'm saying?"

"Look what they did to this place!" Monica

shouted. "They're paying morons like Sked to hunt people down! Let him read the diskette."

She paused, looking hard into her brother's eyes. "Cityweb can't get that diskette, Armitage. You know that."

Armitage nodded slowly, reluctantly. "Grab the computer and take it out on the cabin cruiser, then. Tie up off Ganymede Reach. I'll come out later when I have a better idea what's going on. Hope you know what you're doing, Monica."

7

THE BOAT'S ANCIENT engine gushed heat and noise into the cabin. He glanced out one of the portholes. Monica was steering them away from the pier, heading for the farthest reaches of Watertown. It was safest there, she'd said.

He hit the computer's power switch and the screen glowed amber. He had to concentrate to remember the right commands. He wasn't particularly talented with computers, nothing like Sam, but he knew enough to get by at school. He booted up a word-processing program and gently shoved his brother's diskette into the drive.

There were only two files on the diskette. He tried to call up the first, and an error message flashed at the bottom of the screen. Sam had locked his files.

Paul's heart sank. It was hopeless. Think, think! There was a trick to this. Sam had shown him a few years ago. He used it to copy protected software. But how did it work? He felt a sliver of anger, as if Sam was taunting him: "It's not some great secret, Paul; somewhere in there, the computer knows the code."

His hands felt clumsy against the keyboard. He got into the computer's main operating system and waded into the electronic morass. A daunting matrix of symbols glittered on the monitor: weird arrangements of numbers and letters, exotic flourishes and occult scribbles.

So what's the code, Sam?

His eyes were fixed on the screen. When his memory flagged, he willed his hands to remember the steps for him. The symbols seemed to waver, leap toward him. Perspiration dampened the fringes of his hair. He was rushing through electronic doors, gazing into the labyrinthine innards of the computer. And there it was—Sam's code.

Da Vinci.

The engine cut out as he finished reading the first file. He hadn't understood most of it. There were formulas and molecular models, references to chemical compounds he'd probably never hear about in school. But Sam had added comments and observations in log form, and that part at least, Paul had understood.

Monica's footsteps sounded in the gangway, and he furtively switched off the computer, the text swirling out of sight. He watched her coming into view down the stairs, the scissoring of her legs beneath the bulky pants, the weightless swing of her arms, her thin, pale face.

Why hadn't he suspected? It seemed so obvious now. He'd sensed all along she was different: such power in her frail body, the unnatural speed, the way she always saw and heard things before him. Sked's voice slurred through his head. *Toxic freak. Health hazard.*

"We're tied up off the reach," she said, hesitating on the last step. "What was on the diskette?"

"You drink the water, don't you?"

She looked back at him, silent.

"You drink it, and it changes you." Dead water zone. How could she do that?

"No," she replied, shaking her head. Then again, more firmly, "No!"

He laughed hoarsely, waving his hand at the computer. It was all there.

"No one drinks the water," she insisted, "not anymore. About twenty years ago, everybody did.

But it wasn't so polluted then—that's what my mother said, anyway. Anything bad in it, the Watertowners were immune to, they'd been drinking it for so long. But then the water turned."

"Turned?"

"Changed. People suddenly started getting sick from it, losing weight. Some went crazy, a few died. Almost everyone stopped then. But people who kept drinking it said it wasn't hurting them."

"But it was changing them."

Monica nodded. "Mom said they got real thin, but they got stronger, faster. She was a Waterdrinker."

Paul shook his head in confusion. "But how—"

"I must have got it through Mom, before I was born. Like Armitage. But she wouldn't let us drink it." Her voice suddenly hardened with anger. "Didn't stop her though. Even if it didn't make her sick, it made her go funny. I think that's why she was always wandering off, like she was looking for something. A lot of the other Waterdrinkers disappeared, too. A few of them died, real sudden, all shriveled up, like skeletons—horrible. Anyway, they're all gone now. The kids—most of us banded together on our pier."

"And built a gate to keep people out."

She shrugged. "They hate us, the other Watertowners. A lot of them don't even know about the dead water, but they can all tell we're different. Freaks."

"Not Decks."

"No, Decks is different. He's an old family friend. He never drank the water, but he doesn't hate the people who did. Most Watertowners are more like Sked."

"He seemed almost jealous." Paul remembered the twisted look on the spider boy's face. *Maybe if I had what you all had.*

"I heard he tried to drink the water, but it didn't work for him. Nearly killed him. That's the thing—some people can take it, others can't."

"You never wanted to?" he asked cautiously, remembering her crouched on the pier, the water cupped in her hands.

"No. I told you!" she replied—too loudly, Paul thought. "Anyway, I've got it in me already. And there's nothing I can do about that."

"What does it feel like?" Paul felt rather in awe of her and a little envious, too. She had all the things he'd worked so hard for: speed, strength, agility. He must seem ridiculous, with his heavy, pumped-up muscles.

She shrugged. "It'd be like you trying to describe, say, how your legs feel. This is all I know. I don't have anything to compare it to."

She placed her hand on Paul's bare forearm.

"I feel cold to you?"

Paul nodded, taken aback but strangely excited by this sudden contact.

"You're scalding," she said, puzzled. She brushed her thumb across the underside of his wrist. "Your heart is blasting away." Then she maneuvered his fingers onto her pulse. "Here."

Paul concentrated but felt nothing. A cold prickle moved across his neck. Did she have a pulse at all? But she smiled and pressed his fingers tighter against her skin. He felt something now—not distinct beats, more like a continuous purr.

Paul swallowed. "Yeah, I feel it now."

"We run pretty fast."

He realized he was still holding her wrist and abruptly let go.

"Does it scare you?"

"I don't—no. Is that why you're so pale?"

"I guess so."

"And light?"

"I suppose we don't weigh much, do we? Nothing like you, anyway."

"It makes you tired," he said. "Like after we ran away from Sked."

"Yeah, sometimes it's as if all your energy burns away. But it comes back after a while."

He was trying not to believe any of it—to just stay calm. But Sam had written it all down.

"You knew what would be on the diskette."

"I had an idea."

"Why didn't you tell me?"

"It's not the kind of thing we'd tell strangers, is it?"

"Is that why Armitage didn't want me to read it?"

"One of the reasons. He doesn't want anyone to know about us, especially people from the City. He'd do anything to get the water out of him. He hates it."

"So why did you let me read the diskette?"

"Better you than Cityweb. And," she added with sudden intensity, "I want to know what your brother found. None of the Waterdrinkers ever knew how the dead water worked. They thought it was magic."

"Sam thinks it's some kind of microorganism in the water. He calls it a metabolic accelerator."

"A what?"

"It speeds up the way your body works. It takes over your system."

"Where does it come from?"

"He doesn't know, never saw anything like it. He thinks it might be some kind of mutation, but he couldn't find it on any of his identification tables."

"So it's not magic," she said sadly. She looked

at him defiantly. "You must think I'm some kind of freak."

"No," he said truthfully.

"I wonder. Still, it was only a matter of time before someone found out. Surprised it didn't happen sooner. I don't know what's worse: Cityweb getting hold of it or your brother. What do you think he's going to do with his great discovery?"

Paul felt an icy contraction of fear in his guts. He knew exactly what Sam was planning.

Da Vinci.

The perfect man.

8

SOMETHING WONDERFUL *is going to happen.*

His brother's fevered words sounded in his head as he typed in the code word, calling up the second file. Monica crouched beside him and together they watched as the screen filled with light.

Day 1

I've decided that this is the only way to understand the effects of the dead water on human beings. No amount of computer-simulated modeling can match it. And I want to know. I want to experience it firsthand.

I've screened out all tramp elements and toxic traces from the samples I've collected. I took the first dose at 0800, the second at 1400, and will continue at eight-hour intervals.

No discernible symptoms or observations so far.

"When I first saw him around the old boathouse, I didn't think he was a stranger," said Monica quietly. "I thought he must have been a Waterdrinker—some crazy who didn't know better. You still see them around sometimes."

Paul nodded, mute.

Day 2

Muscle pain. I'm assuming it's an initial reaction to the dead water. Slight fever. Heart rate up. Am continuing the dosage. I'm frightened—should I stop, do more tests, take my data back to the university before going any further?

Some people could take the water, others couldn't— that's what Monica had told him. Which way would it go for his brother? Didn't he know how dangerous it could be?

Day 3

I lifted things today I couldn't have lifted before. At first, the objects seemed too heavy. But then, with some effort, it was possible. I felt as if I was able to instruct my body what to do, redirect all my strength to the active muscles.

Paul thought of his nightmare—Sam, curling barbells, mysteriously strong.

Afterward, fatigue. I slept deeply for two hours. This is in accordance with my theory that the dead water acts as a metabolic accelerator, which fuels the body faster but also exhausts its energy reserves faster.

I continue to take samples from various regions of Watertown in the hopes of learning more about the dead water. Is there a source? What is its exact nature?

Day 4

A thrum. A buzz in my head. It's always there in the background. It changes when you move, altering pitch with every motion of your body. It is sensitive to other things, too: when something enters your field of vision, when an object moves around you.

A bird flew into the boathouse through a window and panicked, swooping madly through the air. I watched until it flew close to me, and then my hands darted out with perfect timing and caught it gently. I don't know who was more surprised—the bird or me.

"Do you have that?" Paul asked. "A sound in your head?"

"I'd never thought of it like that before. There's a part of me that can tell when something's going to happen. Say I step on a rotten piece of wood. I can feel it start to give before it actually does. Or when I pickpocket someone, I can tell when the person's body has noticed, even before his brain has. But it always comes like a sound in my head."

My eyesight has also improved dramatically. With my glasses on, things seemed slightly skewed at first; now everything is distorted. The lenses are overcompensating. I don't need them.

You just left them behind, thought Paul. Nobody abducted you. You just discarded what you didn't need. But your clothes, what about them?

I feel as if I'm being recalibrated, remade. I've been losing weight. My clothes barely fit. At first, this upset me, but now I can't help finding it exhilarating and liberating! When I was younger, I thought what I wanted was to be bigger, heavier, with more muscle and fat to insulate me against the world. But now I see that weight works against you, pulls you down to the earth. Refined to the bare essentials, with less weight, you can see, hear, feel things more intensely!

What was he doing to himself? Paul touched the keys, and more text climbed the screen.

Day 5

Waking, I was aware of my body as never before. I could feel every artery pumping blood out of my heart, every vein bringing it back. In my mind's eye, I saw the configuration of my tissue and muscle, sinew and bone. With concentration I could sense my cells dividing, multiplying, feel the work going on within me, like a piece of miraculous machinery! Just lying still, listening to my body, I'm learning things—things no textbook or lab experiment could teach.

"He's gone past us," Monica breathed. "I haven't felt those things, not ever."

"You're sure?"

"Yeah. I only got the water secondhand. He's taking it directly. It's bound to make him change, fast."

Paul fought back the spasm of fear in his stomach. How far would Sam take this experiment on his own body?

Day 6

They're looking for me. I've seen an unmarked helicopter circling Watertown. There are two men—one was at the lab when the City issued special security clearances for the project. They must have found something I left behind. I can't believe I was so careless. What? Some scribbled notes retrieved and reassembled from the paper shredder? They can't know very much—but enough to trace me here. What do they want? My findings? My findings destroyed?

I followed them one night as they moved nervously through Watertown. I felt like a wraith, sliding in and out of shadow effortlessly, pressing my body into alcoves, flat against walls. They have a picture of me and showed it to a punk in black leather. One of the men gave him money.

I can't be interrupted now. I'm not finished yet. I've grown much thinner, much stronger and quicker, but that's become almost insignificant. There's something much more important to be done. But first I have to keep taking it into me. And I must find out where the primary source is.

Day 7

I go out only at night now. Daylight hurts my eyes. Too much stimulus. I can travel across Watertown alone, soaring across rooftops like a dream. I never knew that the light changes throughout the night, the spin of the moon and stars. You can hear more clearly, too. Always the sound of the boats, night crews on deck handling metal and rope, voices drifting. I have listened to fish beneath the water's surface, insects sleeping, the sound of the mist gathering in the night.

"So, it *was* Sam," Paul whispered. But why had he appeared, only to run away? Twice. Why hadn't he stayed to explain? And the inevitable conclusion: he didn't want to see me.

Day 8

I think I've found the source.

Wandering deeper into Watertown, taking samples, I found a wide canal that encircles a kind of citadel island. The dead water is more potent here. The surrounding area seems deserted. Why?

I'm worried the helicopter men will track me to the boathouse if I wait any longer. I need somewhere safe to carry on the rest of my experiment undisturbed. It's time to move on. I'm certain the source lies beyond that canal.

Paul hammered at the keyboard, but he'd reached the end. There were no more words.

"Rat Castle," said Monica, in amazement. "No wonder Mom wandered around there. She must have been drinking from that damn canal."

"Sam's in there."

"But Decks said—"

"Decks was wrong."

"She might be there, too, then," said Monica quietly. "With that much dead water in her, she could have jumped right across."

Paul stood up quickly. "We've got to go there."

Monica took a deep breath. "No. Not yet. It's too dangerous."

"But we're wasting time!"

"Paul, I want to go, too. But it's still light out. At nightfall Armitage'll come and tell us what's happening with Cityweb."

"Sam hates his body! He'd do anything to change it, even if it might kill him." He faltered for a moment. "Because he knows he's going to die anyway."

"But why?"

"It's part of his condition. They say he'll only live another twelve years maximum, probably less."

"Oh." She seemed to draw into herself, then said bitterly, "So he thinks he can heal himself with the water."

Paul nodded. "When he called me, he was

scared. I think he wanted me to come here and stop him. Why else would he have called? I owe him this." He studied her face, suddenly needing to tell her. "I let him down."

"How?"

"The stupidest thing I've ever done. We weren't the same afterward. And then he left for college and it still wasn't fixed. Isn't."

"Tell me."

"Lick it up," Randy Smith said.

Pinned to the ground, Sam just stared back.

"Make him lick it up!" Randy shouted. Gavin and Peter grabbed Sam by the hair and forced his face toward the glistening puddle of Randy's saliva.

"Randy, come on!" Paul shouted, but they held him tight.

"Shut up and watch." Randy grinned. "This is for your viewing pleasure."

They'd been ambushed on their way home from school. They'd been taking the secret route through the park for months, but Randy had found out and was waiting with a whole bunch of his friends.

Peter and Gavin dragged Sam's face into the spittle, but his lips were clamped tight. He tried to raise a hand to wipe his cheek, but they restrained him.

Randy prodded him in the ribs with his sneaker. "Forget it," he said. "We like you like this. Don't you think it suits him?" he asked the crowd. Laughter.

Paul looked around in revulsion. "That's enough!"

Randy looked at him with interest. "You love it, Paul. Admit it, you love seeing this."

Paul caught his brother's eye, but Sam looked away.

"There's not much to him, is there?" Randy said. "Let's see how little there really is."

Sam started to struggle again. Paul couldn't bear the panic in his eyes.

"Randy, that's enough, damn it!" he yelled. He struggled with all his might, but the three boys holding him only clamped down tighter.

"Paul, you've always wanted this," said Randy.

Gavin and Peter were ripping Sam's shirt. Paul watched, mesmerized. They pulled away the tattered fabric, exposing Sam's pale chest. Then they dragged his naked, firepole arms over his head so that he looked even skinnier, skeletal.

"Look at his arms!"

"His chest's weird!"

"His jeans," Randy said.

"No," Paul mumbled. "No!"

When they were finished, Sam was stripped down to his underwear, lying on his side, his knees pulled up to his chest.

"Sam, you okay?"

Sam stood up, his back to Paul, and dragged his jeans on. He arranged the tatters of his T-shirt over his shoulders and walked away.

"Sam." Paul followed at a slight distance. "Sam, I tried."

Sam kept walking.

"They held me back."

"There was nothing you could've done," said Monica.

He wanted to believe her. Nothing he could have done. But he'd come too far with the truth now. "I told Randy Smith where we'd be. I told him to wait there for us."

She didn't say anything.

"I didn't plan it, not really." He studied her face, trying to decipher the look in her piercing eyes. "He was so pleased to be going away to college, so happy to be leaving Governor's Hill. It shouldn't have made me so angry, but I felt like he'd forgotten all the things I did for him, taking care of him. None of it was important to him anymore."

"So how did it happen?"

"I was in the locker room after swim practice one day, and Randy was there, and they started baiting me about Sam. Usually it's like flashes of dark colors in my head. But this time, I just started agreeing with them. And the more they went on, the angrier I got—not with them but with Sam. I just blurted out about our secret way home from school. He was going to wait there for us. He'd give Sam a scare, that was all, maybe a few shoves. That was our deal."

"Randy broke it. Not you."

"Well, I was an idiot to believe him, wasn't I? Paul—who suddenly trusts the enemy." The enemy. *You love this, Paul. Admit it, you love seeing this.* And somewhere deep inside him, a very quiet voice had replied, Yes, I do.

"Did Sam know it was you?"

"No. But he still blames me. When I came down here, I was hoping I could somehow fix things between us." He combed his fingers restlessly through his hair, suddenly assailed by doubts. "But it's been so long now. Maybe he doesn't want me here at all; maybe I just imagined it to make myself feel important. How can I convince him to stop taking the water? What would I say?"

Monica stood and lit an old oil lantern hanging from the ceiling.

"I don't know what I'd say if I found my mom.

I'd probably be angry as hell. Leaving us like that. Aw, who knows what I'd say." She flung out her hands in a gesture of contempt. "I'd ask her some things, I guess. Why'd she keep on drinking the water? She knew it was making her crazy, but she kept on anyway!"

She sat down beside Paul, her body rigid, looking fiercely at the wall.

"Maybe I wouldn't have anything to say at all," she went on more quietly. "What it really came down to is simple—she was more interested in drinking the dead water than sticking around. She wasn't even much of a mother. I'm still looking though. Stupid, isn't it?"

Paul took her cool hand in his. He'd never simply touched someone out of sympathy before, and it surprised him. He could feel her cat's pulse beneath her pale skin. In the warm light from the lantern she was like something from a fairy tale, thin and airy, with dark, streaming hair. Had he really thought she was ugly?

She turned to him with a quizzical look, and he almost lost his nerve. He could pull back his hand. But he didn't want to, and he felt as if some disconnected part of him was making the decisions.

He awkwardly curved a hand behind her slender neck and kissed her on the mouth. He felt clumsy; he was probably doing it wrong. But she tasted warm and salty as she kissed him back. He encircled her with his arms and felt her pickpocket's hands pressing into his back. All at once it seemed so obvious that this should be happening, and he was laughing quietly, and she was, too. He drew back to look into her face, brushing his fingertips over her cheekbones and eyebrows.

He pressed his face into her hair, breathing its warm perfume, wanting to be swallowed up by it. Nothing mattered except this.

But she suddenly stiffened.

"What is it?" he asked, embarrassed and confused.

With a swift movement, she reached up and extinguished the lantern.

"There's someone walking along the pier," she said from the sudden darkness.

9

PAUL KNOCKED ASIDE the ragged curtains and peered out into the night. At first he saw only the long, dark line of the pier, shrouded in mist. But after a few moments, his eyes adjusted, and he spotted a vertical brushstroke of darkness blending with the water and the distant buildings.

"There's three of them," breathed Monica, looking over his shoulder.

As Paul continued to stare, he saw a second dark form and a third, walking in line down the pier.

"It's Sked and his fun friends," Monica said, letting the curtains fall back into place. "They don't usually hang out around here."

"They can't be looking for us," Paul muttered.

"It's time to leave."

Paul hurried on deck after her. The cool of the night air made him shiver.

"Cast us off," Monica whispered from the wheel.

He reached over the side and fumbled with the knot. The engine kicked over with a noisy wheeze, then died. Fingers tugging numbly at the painter, he looked anxiously down the pier. They'd been spotted. Sked and his friends were running now, their boots thudding against the planking. For a second time the engine roared to life, racing for a few seconds before sputtering out. Monica swore.

Paul clawed at the knot, his hands trembling. He worked a strand loose. Come on! The boat's motor growled uncertainly and then strengthened.

"We're gone!" Monica shouted. The cabin cruiser lurched away from the pier, throwing Paul across the deck.

"It's still tied!" he cried out.

The boat heaved back, the painter taut as a tightrope. Sked was almost at the pier's edge, and he jumped. With a whip's crack, the painter ripped the metal cleat out of the pier, and the boat surged ahead. Not quickly enough. Paul watched in horror as Sked sailed through the air and landed on deck in a clumsy crouch. Paul tried to scramble out of the way, but Sked brought a steel-toed boot down on his hand. Swearing, he butted his whole body against Sked's legs, knocking him against the boat's railing.

"Get him off!" he heard Monica yell. Her voice sounded a long way away.

He pushed himself quickly to his feet and faced Sked. "All alone, aren't you? No friends this time." His voice was trembling, but he noticed that Sked looked uncertain.

"You're swimming home, Sked."

The spider boy laughed—a shrill, demented hooting that sent terror through Paul. Then Sked lunged. He clamped one thick hand around Paul's windpipe, the other onto his ear, as if trying to rip it off his head. The searing pain paralyzed Paul for a second. He felt himself gag for breath. Light bloomed in the corners of his eyes—a bright, desperate purple. Very detached, he realized he was being strangled. Sked was trying to kill him. He was looking into Sked's fevered, pockmarked face, smelling his breath. He was going to die.

His vision wavered, and for a moment he was looking into the face of Randy Smith. With a sudden rage he drove his numb fist into Sked's chin, and the hands loosened. Paul felt a burst of dark, intense pleasure. He lashed out again, punching Sked in the stomach, winding him. The hands fell away from his throat and ear. Another punch in the face sent Sked staggering back. Paul danced forward and struck him again. He realized he was bellowing, a deep guttural roar racking his throat. He could feel the superb strength of his body, wanting to break bones, see blood.

He pinned Sked to the deck by sitting on his legs. He caught him around the neck with both hands, squeezing.

"How's that?" he shouted feverishly into the spider boy's face. "How does that feel?"

Sked's fingers tried to pry away his hands, but Paul held tight, tighter.

"Just get him off, Paul!"

The spell was broken. Paul looked down at Sked, took hold of his leather jacket, and half dragged, half lifted him toward the side of the boat.

"You're dead!" Sked screeched hoarsely, and then he was laughing again. "They're going to get you! You are *dead*!"

Paul shoved him backward into the night water and watched him flailing about until he was swallowed by the mist. He dropped to his knees. It hurt to swallow, and there was a faint ringing in his right ear. Several fingers were already swollen around the joints, and he could only bend them halfway. His stomach lurched and he made it to the railing just in time. He'd been ready to kill Sked—he would have done it. A second wave of nausea swept over him.

A hand rested gently on the back of his neck. "You all right?"

He spat to clear his mouth, waiting for his breathing to smooth out.

"I thought you were going to kill him."

"Me, too."

"I would have stopped sooner, but I saw another boat. I just wanted to get as far away as possible." She took his hands carefully between hers. They felt cool and soothing against his burning skin.

"Your brother set us up," he rasped.

She stared into the mist.

"He was the only one who knew where we were! Monica, are you listening to me?"

"I'm listening," she replied, her voice expressionless.

"He told Cityweb where to find us! They wanted to kill us! Both of us! Why'd Armitage do that?"

"I don't know."

"Your own brother!"

"I don't know why he did it, all right? He's got

112

his own reasons, probably. You can't trust anyone, not even family. They all betray you in the end! Look what you did to your brother!"

"That's not fair! It's not the same!"

She wasn't listening. "Everyone does it to everyone else. You should never trust anyone!" She was raging through her tears now. "You should never put yourself in a position to lose! I was stupid to get involved in any of this," she muttered in disgust. "Look at us!" She flung out her thin hands at the fog. "This is a loser's situation."

"Where are we?"

She sighed, jamming her hands into her pockets. "Out in the shipping lanes."

Foghorns sounded mournfully across the water, seemingly from all directions at once, soft, strengthening, then fading.

Paul gazed anxiously into the impenetrable mist. "Is it safe out here?"

"Where is it safe for us? You tell me and I'll take us there. Cityweb's probably paid off everyone in Watertown by now. They want us dead, Paul!"

"What they really want is the diskette. They think it'll lead them to Sam."

"Your brother found out some secret and they don't want anyone to know about it. Whatever it is, it's worth killing people for."

"We've got to get to Sam first."

Monica turned away from him. "You can get out of this, you know." She spoke quickly, as if trying to convince herself. "I could dump you in the docklands. You could catch a train back to where you came from."

Escape: leave everything behind. Watertown. Cityweb. Sam. Forget it all.

"It's impossible," he told her softly.

"It's out of our control!"

"I've got to find him."

"Your brother's made his choice," she said fiercely. "You don't owe him anything! It's stupid, thinking that way! Why do you have to take these risks for him?"

"Because I'm nothing without him!" The words welled up from deep inside him, unbidden—his brother's words, traveling across time.

Monica was staring at him, her body tensed with the force of his voice. He was breathing hard, as if he'd just done fifty push-ups. He looked away from her, into the mist.

"After I set him up, I thought it would be a relief when he went to college. But the guilt didn't go away. And I missed him, bad. When I was working out, I'd wonder what the point was. There was nobody to look after. I felt like an obsolete piece of machinery. You know how people lose an arm or a leg and still feel pain in that empty space? That's what it was like, having him gone."

He knew now what had driven him to Watertown. Not worry, not guilt. It was need. He needed Sam.

She nodded slowly and for a few moments said nothing. Then, "Do you think she's in there, too? My mother?"

"I don't know," he said carefully. "Maybe."

"I'm not sure how to get inside. It's all bricks and boards and iron gates. We'll need some pretty heavy tools."

He touched her arm. "Thanks."

She sniffed the air suddenly and turned to the back of the boat. "Piece of garbage," she muttered in disgust. "Should have known the damn thing would seize up! Look!"

Paul turned with her to see a few tendrils of black smoke coming through the planking. Monica shut the engine down and yanked open the hatch, leaning back as dense fumes ballooned into the night air.

"This is not a good place to be dead in the water," she said grimly. "Get the tools."

He hefted out the toolbox. Monica was already lowering herself into the hatch, coughing away the smoke. A foghorn blasted nearby, and Paul could make out a huge cliff of metal sliding slowly through the mist. It wasn't coming toward them, but he knew it wouldn't be long before one did.

"How's it going?" he asked after a few minutes.

"Not good. There's parts all melted together."

"You can do it."

"No." She hauled herself out of the hatch. "It's fried."

"You're giving up?"

She offered him the hammer. "You want to try?"

"We're going to get rammed if we stay out here!"

The mist swirled around the cabin cruiser, then opened to reveal the shape of a small motor-boat drifting toward them. He half raised his arm to wave it off, but Monica stopped him.

"That's the boat I saw at Ganymede Reach."

It glided closer. Paul could make out two figures on board. "Cityweb," he said, helpless.

"No," she said. "Armitage. And Decks."

10

"YOU SNAKE!" spat Monica as the motorboat came alongside. Armitage tried to grab hold of the railing, but Monica kicked his hands away.

"Listen to me!" he yelled up at her. "This isn't my fault!"

For a few seconds Paul could only stare, the hammer clenched in his right hand.

"Not your fault?" he shouted at Armitage. "You called them. You told them where to find us! Sked and his friends just tried to kill us!"

"Put down the hammer, Paul," said Decks calmly.

"And you, too," Monica whispered at Decks.

"No." Armitage shook his head. "Decks has nothing to do with it. They planted a bug on me."

"What are you talking about?" demanded Monica.

Armitage offered her a coil of rope. "Look, tie us up; let us come on board."

"No," Paul said. "What do you mean, they had a bug on you?"

Armitage sighed. "I'm one of their spooks."

Paul saw the shocked disbelief on Monica's face.

"Around the time Mom disappeared, they snared me in the docklands. They knew all about the business. I was this close to getting taken in. But they made me an offer. If I spooked for them in Watertown, they'd look the other way. Said they needed people out here."

"They own you!" Monica said with contempt. "You sold yourself—and me, too. You had no right to do that!"

"I was protecting us!" Armitage said impatiently. "Can't you see that? They would have shut us down in a second! You'd be in some detention home in the suburbs right now!"

"So instead we've got glue-sniffing punks after us! Big improvement, Armitage!"

"I didn't know they'd go this far!"

"You knew all along they were looking for my brother, didn't you?" Paul asked. "Even before I showed up."

Armitage shrugged. "I'm sorry, Paul. I really am. But this was business, and I didn't know you—didn't know why they wanted your brother. It wasn't my problem."

"No wonder you let me stay," Paul muttered, ashamed of his naïveté. "You told them about the boathouse. And you were going to give them the diskette, too, weren't you?"

"Just trying to stay afloat, like I said." He was staring down at his shoes, but when he looked back up, there was a spark of anger dancing in his eyes. "I tried to buy you some time, Paul. Maybe you don't realize that. I come back from the docklands and find my place wrecked. And then you suddenly tell me your brother's been doing research on the water"—his eyes darted to Monica—"so I'm beginning to wonder what's so important about that diskette, and thinking that maybe we'd better read it before anyone else does. I wasn't trying to set you up on Ganymede Reach. They must have bugged me this morning. I didn't find out until I went to see Decks. It triggered his alarm system. Took us about half an hour to find the damn thing in my clothes."

"We came out to the reach as fast as we could," Decks continued. "We thought we saw you heading out into the shipping lanes. I'm amazed we found you in all this fog."

"Yeah, well, the engine's packed it in," sighed Monica.

"First things first, then," said Decks. "They'll come looking in that helicopter of theirs before long. We've got to get you out of here."

"We can rig a towline maybe," Armitage suggested.

"Too slow," said Monica. "Anyway, they'll be looking for this boat."

"Burn it," said Paul, amazed at his audacity.

Armitage stared, taken aback. "A bit excessive, don't you think? You have any idea how much it would cost to replace a boat like this?"

"Paul's right," said Monica firmly. "We set it on fire, and if we're lucky, they think we had an accident in the shipping lanes. There's some gasoline below deck."

"We could replace the engine," moaned Armitage. "It's a perfectly good boat."

"Make it fast," Decks said to Paul.

Paul hurried down into the cabin, Monica close behind. He hesitated at the computer and pulled Sam's diskette from the drive. Prying open the plastic casing with his fingernails, he tore at the flimsy vinyl surface beneath until it was shredded. There. No one else would get hold of it now.

A gasoline canister was being pressed into his hands. Hastily he unscrewed the cap and doused the floor, the bunks, the wooden walls of the hull. He paused to push open all the portholes on either side of the cabin.

"For a good draft," he explained when he caught Monica's look of astonishment.

"How d'you know about stuff like this?" she asked.

"TV."

She almost laughed. "I'm going above to do the deck."

Paul could scarcely believe that only a few days ago he'd been in Governor's Hill, crossing at crosswalks (never against the red light), giving back change that had mistakenly been given to him, holding open supermarket doors for elderly people. Now, here he was spurting gasoline around like a seasoned arsonist. Dumping out the last of his canister he hurried up the stairs, gulping in the fresh air.

"I'm almost done," Monica told him. "Get off."

He swung himself over the railing and hopped into the motorboat. He peered into the fog, expecting a tanker to loom up at any moment or a helicopter's spotlight to impale them.

"Hurry," he called to her.

"I can't believe I'm letting this happen," Armitage mumbled.

Monica dropped lightly over the side, holding two rags and a box of matches. She lit the first rag, allowed it to burn for a few seconds and then tossed it up onto the deck. A carpet of low flames spread across the planking. The second burning rag she pushed through the nearest porthole.

"Let's go!" she cried out, pushing off from the hull.

Deep orange light blossomed from the cabin, and a hungry sucking noise filled the air. The motorboat's engine roared to life, and Armitage veered them away. A loud crackling and popping carried across the water. Paul watched as the mist closed in. Only a diffuse orange glow indicated where the boat lay, burning.

"I hereby pronounce you both officially dead," said Armitage. "My boat, too."

"We're going to my place," Decks told them. "You'll all be safe there for a while."

Armitage looked at Paul. "So, you planning on telling us what was on the diskette?"

"Everything about the water," Monica replied simply.

Armitage nodded slowly. "I thought it might be that." He turned around to look Paul intently in the eye. "You know we don't drink it."

It seemed desperately important to him, and Paul nodded quickly. He could sense Armitage's shame and felt embarrassed and guilty, a clumsy trespasser in these people's lives.

"I know. Monica explained it to me."

"It has nothing to do with us," Armitage went on angrily. "It was Mom's mistake. She drank it; we inherited it. Simple as that. I wouldn't drink that crap for anything."

"My brother's drinking it," Paul said.

A small groan escaped Armitage's throat, a combination of surprise and weariness. "Why?"

"He wants to make himself perfect."

"Then he might already be dead by now," said Decks quietly. "It works differently on different people."

"No," said Monica, staring into the distance. "It took with him. He said so on the diskette."

"We know where he is, too," said Paul. "Rat Castle."

Decks's brow furrowed. "You're certain?"

"The place on the other side of the canal," said Paul, frightened by the intensity of the man's gaze. "He said he was going there because the water was stronger."

"It's the truth, Decks," said Monica. "And if he's in there"—her voice gained momentum—"it means there could be other people in there—"

"No," said Decks abruptly, cutting her off, "there's no one there."

"How can you know that?"

"It's just not possible," he replied, his voice tired. "Not anymore, not after what the Sturms did to themselves."

Monica looked at Paul. "They were the first convict family to stay behind after the prison hulks were closed down."

"You can't blame them really," Decks began slowly. "From what I've heard, most of the convicts didn't deserve to be imprisoned. They hated the City for what it had done to them. It was a rage, like a phosphorus burn. Do you know about phosphorus? It ignites when it's exposed to the air. If it gets on your flesh, there's no way of stopping it burning. Water's no good. It just goes on forever."

Paul wondered if it was this same kind of rage that drove his brother—the fury of being crippled, ashamed, wanting revenge on everyone, the world.

"They wanted power," Decks went on. "And they got it, in a way. They made themselves the new rulers of Watertown. They controlled all the inner piers, the canals, trade routes across the harbor. To rival the City—that was their dream. They wanted to spread their power right into the heart of the City. But the City made it illegal for anyone to trade with Watertown. That crushed them."

"They went at it the wrong way," said Armitage in a tight voice. "Playing by the rules won't get you anywhere, not against the City. They make the rules to protect themselves. So you've got to break them if you want to get strong. Be patient, secret. That's the way they should have worked."

"Maybe so," said Decks, "but the Sturm family was crushed. In only a few years all their power had ebbed away. The family turned in on itself, living isolated in Rat Castle.

"But when the water turned, the last of the Sturms thought it might be another chance for them. They discovered what the water could do to people and what's more, that the water around Rat Castle was the strongest of all. That's why the walls went up. The Sturms wanted that dead water for themselves only. And they started playing with it."

Decks paused to spit into the water, as if his words left a foul taste in his mouth. His broad fingers scratched thoughtfully at the stubble on his chin.

"Nobody knew where the dead water came from or what it was. The Sturms didn't have a clue what they were doing. Some drank too much; others made concoctions that killed them before they'd finished swallowing. Most of those who survived were half crazy from it. They were nothing like the other Waterdrinkers, who drank only from the outer piers. You might not even think they were human.

"The Sturms were killed off by it, except for two brothers. David, the oldest, was hell-bent on refining it so that it wouldn't kill you but would make you stronger, faster. He wanted to make himself into an invincible being, a god."

Paul's scalp tingled. Exactly what Sam was after. He had to hear the rest. But Decks hesitated, as if reluctant to continue.

"There was a falling out between the brothers," he began carefully, "and the younger one left Rat Castle. You can't understand the pull of the dead water, even the weakest of it. Once people drank, it was almost impossible for them to stop."

"Like Mom," said Monica quietly.

"She fought against it, your mother, but she couldn't stop."

"You know what happened to her, don't you?"

"Waterdrinkers, like your mother, were aware of what went on in Rat Castle. They needed the stronger water. David Sturm would use them to test his new potions. It was unholy what he did to them."

Paul winced in revulsion. The expression on Monica's face made his heart contract.

"You knew all along!" she whispered. "She

might still be there!"

"Now listen," said Decks kindly but firmly, "these are terrible things to hear, I know. I watched your mother fighting against the water, and when she disappeared, I went to Rat Castle myself. You must believe me when I tell you she wasn't there, Monica. There was no one there." A sigh escaped his lips, misting in the night air. "The dead water wasn't meant to be drunk. The final experiments must have killed anyone who was left."

"Whenever I asked you about Rat Castle," she said evenly, fighting emotion, "you always warned me away. Why? What would I have found?"

"I was afraid for you," replied Decks. "I was afraid you'd feel the lure of the water, too. Your mother said it was like a sound, a song in her head. That's how powerful it was, don't you see? I didn't want the same thing to happen to you."

"You never saw her dead?" Monica asked, insistent.

"No."

"Then you can't be sure, can you? Maybe they were hiding."

"I can't believe that," Decks muttered, more to himself than anyone else. "David was already half dead when I last saw him—"

Paul stared at him, stunned. "You're the younger brother."

Decks looked back in silence.

Monica was shaking her head in disbelief. "No, it's not true. I remember you when I was little. You lived in the houseboat. You weren't a Waterdrinker. Mom said you tried—"

"But it didn't take with me. I couldn't share what they had. So maybe there was jealousy in me. But I left Rat Castle over twelve years ago, not long after David began his experiments. I went back from time to time, to plead with him to stop. Each time, there were fewer people and he was more mad and wizened. The last time I saw him—a few months before your mother disappeared—I knew he couldn't last much longer." Decks hesitated but then continued in a forceful voice. "And it's right that he died. It's right that the experiments are over, because the water's evil." He raised his finger at Paul. "And if this brother of yours is doing the same work, he may end up dead long before Cityweb finds him."

"Can you show me the way inside?"

"You want to save him, do you?" said Decks softly. "But ask yourself this: does he want to be saved? I tried with David. Once he's taken the water in abundance, you won't be able to stop him."

"Yes I will." What did Decks know about it? He didn't know Sam, didn't know either of them, their whole history together. Sam wanted him here: he'd telephoned; he'd haunted Paul through Watertown! At night on the pier, he'd come to watch Paul through the stilt-house window. How could Decks possibly understand?

"Try to understand what I'm going to say," Decks said. "I think it would be best if we let him be."

"Let him kill himself?" asked Paul incredulously.

"He's made his choice."

"Say we did leave him," said Paul as calmly as possible. "Cityweb will find him eventually. And if it's something they really want to cover up, they won't kill just Sam; they'll kill everyone who knows about the dead water. All of us, everyone who has the water in them. I'm not asking anyone to go with me. Just show me the way inside!"

"I'm going, too," said Monica.

"She won't be there," Armitage sneered. "Haven't you been listening to Decks? She's dead."

"I want to see this place for myself!" Her eyes were bright and hard.

"Is that all you can think about? Don't you see what's going on around you? Our business is ruined, Monica! Cityweb's going to shut me down. Everything I've worked for, gone!"

Monica looked down at the bottom of the boat. "This is important to me, Armitage. Understand, please."

"No, I don't understand," he snapped angrily, but Paul thought he heard his voice quaver. "I was trying to hold things together, and she was off wandering, looking for the perfect fix. She didn't care. But I cared, and now everything's coming apart!"

"I'm sorry," she said. "Really, I am."

But Armitage just glared ahead into the mist, steering them back to Watertown.

"You'll show us, won't you, Decks?" Monica asked.

"If that's what it really takes to bury this, I'll take you both in," said Decks grimly. He turned to Paul. "You may find your brother, but I'm warning you—you won't recognize what he's become."

11

With a rusty shriek, the gate swung slowly back.

Long strands of bulbous green weed trailed from the huge pilings, fanning out across the dark water. The jagged ends of dock spikes bristled from the cross timbers, impaling the gloom. Paul grimaced as the pungent smell of oil and rot wafted over him. There was about five feet of clearance, he guessed, between the water and the underside of the planking above. He looked dubiously at Monica and took a deep breath—so this was the way inside.

Decks had guided them into the heart of Watertown through a maze of canals, some so narrow that the dinghy had caught against the sides.

The mist had started to brighten as they'd glided into the moat, using the oars to skirt around the wood and metal ramparts of Rat Castle. When Decks brought the boat to a halt, he brushed his hands over a section of wall, scraping away debris with his fingernails until he'd exposed a keyhole.

"Stay with the boat," he told Armitage now, as he pushed a ring of keys back into a pocket. "Take it into one of the canals for shelter if need be, but for heaven's sake, keep an eye out for us. Now, steady the boat for me."

The wiry man crouched in the dinghy, then stepped quickly into the opening. Paul followed, easing himself onto a narrow crossbeam, hunched over. The wood was slippery, carpeted with lake fungus, and his hands reached out for balance.

"Hey," he heard Armitage whisper behind him. "Hope you find your brother."

Paul looked awkwardly back over his shoulder.

"Thanks."

Armitage's gaze shifted uncertainly to his sister. It seemed to Paul that he was about to say something, but in the end, he only mumbled, "Be careful, okay?"

Paul shuffled along the beam to make room for Monica.

She stepped lightly from the boat, hardly

rocking it at all. He extended his hand to her and was grateful that she took it, even though she didn't need his help. She smiled at him, but it was forced, her eyes dark and secretive.

Up ahead, Decks was gesturing to them to hurry up. Cautiously Paul moved forward. The timbers groaned ominously, only inches above the water.

"There used to be houses lining this pier," said Decks in a muted voice, jabbing a finger upward. "Not like the shacks you see most places in Watertown now. Some of these houses were quite grand. My family certainly had its day. But even when I was young, this place was well on its way to ruin. The last time I saw David, he'd left the family home altogether and moved back onto the ship."

"Ship?"

"The last of the convict hulks."

"But I thought they'd all sunk!" said Monica. "Years ago!"

Decks shook his head. "David had this one hauled out onto one of the docks. That must have been almost thirty years ago. He wanted it preserved, like a museum piece, so we wouldn't forget our heritage. When I was last here though, part of the dock had collapsed, and the ship's stern was slumped in the water. Could be that it's slipped back completely by now. We'll see."

Paul followed Decks through the decaying latticework of beams, trying to match the wiry man's footsteps. But his feet slithered on the timbers, and twice he lost his balance and nearly plunged a flailing hand onto one of the spikes. His neck ached from hunching over and his hands throbbed hotly beneath the bandages he'd put on at Decks's houseboat. He couldn't give in to fatigue now; he couldn't fail Sam. He needed to be strong.

His thoughts raced ahead. He tried to plan out a confession, linking words and sentences like paper chains. But was an apology enough? And if he couldn't even be sure that Sam would forgive him, how could he convince him to stop drinking the dead water? Stop, he told himself. Just get there.

There was less space between the beams now, and at times he had to slip through sideways; but after a few more minutes, the timbers became even more tightly meshed into a narrow opening about two feet in diameter, close to the water's surface.

"It's tight," Decks said over his shoulder, "but I've done it before."

The wood was wet and unpleasantly spongy against Paul's hands and knees. He tried to take shallow breaths; he didn't even want to breathe a molecule of that water. He hunched his broad shoulders as he crawled into the opening. Splinters of metal tugged at his clothing. One shoulder lodged tight against a timber. His shoes skittered along the beam, hoping for traction. He was stuck.

He'd never thought of himself as overweight before coming to Watertown. He felt ridiculous; he almost laughed. He tried to wriggle free, but he wasn't going anywhere. He was suddenly short of breath, imagining himself bound by steel hoops, tightening, collapsing the life out of him.

"Monica," he whispered. "I can't move."

"You're all right," she said behind him. "We've just got to ease you through."

A cool tongue lapped across his fingers, and he looked down with a start. The dark water was level with the beam.

"Water," he managed.

"Tide's coming up," said Decks, in front. "I'm reaching back, Paul."

He watched for Decks's hand and grabbed hold. He felt himself shift slightly, but he still wasn't free.

"Again," said Decks, and Paul pulled with all his might.

"No good," he panted, looking at the water,

only a few inches away. Would it lick against his chest, fill his mouth and nostrils? He felt Monica's small, cool hands against his ankles and was reassured.

"Once more," she said.

Paul took a deep breath and yanked hard on Decks's arm, just as Monica shoved him from behind. He jerked out of the wooden stranglehold and had to cling to the beam to stop himself from going into the water. He scrambled out of the tunnel and pushed himself to his feet, his knees shaking.

"Okay?" Monica asked, standing behind him.

"Saved me again," he said weakly. "Thanks."

"Can you hear it?" she asked abruptly. "It sounds so clear." She cocked her head to one side. "The water."

Decks nodded dolefully. "Your mother could hear it, too."

"What's it like?" asked Paul.

"Mosquitoes, sort of. But higher."

There was a look of bewildered fascination on Monica's face that made him nervous. He wanted to shake her. What if Decks was right about the lure of the water? They shouldn't have let her come. It was too dangerous.

"Come on," said Decks, "it's not far now."

In the distance, Paul could see pale light

between the pilings. He picked out his footing with care as the water rose. Finally, he was at the far side, and he jumped from the timbers onto a landing platform floating at the pier's base. They were on the edge of another canal.

Through the ragged swaths of mist Paul made out the form of a ship across the canal. The dark bulk of it towered above him, the pockmarked hull stretched taut over wooden ribs, like mummified skin.

As if stirring from sleep, the entire hulk shifted slightly, and a moan issued from the chains draped across its hull. Gooseflesh broke out across Paul's forearms, even though he told himself it was just a dead ship, rolling with the tide.

"Still afloat," said Decks in a whisper. "It must be lashed tight to the wharf."

"There." Monica pointed to the hulk. "The water. It's coming from there."

For a moment, Paul thought he heard a shrill mosquito droning, but it quickly faded.

"If your brother was looking for the source, that's where he'd find it."

"Take the ladder to the pier," said Decks, pointing. "There's a bridge across to the other side."

Paul hurried up the ladder after Monica. But the third rung gave way beneath his foot, and he plunged back to the landing stage, knocking Decks in a heap.

He helped Decks up. "I should have learned by now," he said, mortified. "Are you hurt?"

"No, I'm fine, fine."

Paul was about to try the ladder again when he saw something lying on the ground at Decks's feet. His heart raced. He heard Decks's grunt of surprise and knew he was staring at it, too.

"What's the gun for, Decks?"

"Just a precaution."

"Against what? Cityweb?"

"That, too. Now listen, Paul. When I last saw David, he was violent, dangerous. He nearly killed me."

"You said he was dead."

"I believe he is."

"It's for Sam, isn't it?"

"I didn't say that. But when you see him—if you see him—you might be glad I brought this."

"No," said Paul, shaking his head dazedly. "No." The idea that Decks had a gun and was willing to use it on Sam sparked a short circuit of pure panic through him. He kicked at the gun, hoping to knock it into the water, but it just skittered farther down the landing stage, and Decks ran after it. Paul heaved himself up the ladder, frantically smashing out the rungs behind him.

"No one's going to hurt him!" Paul yelled, kicking at the side struts.

"Helicopter!"

Paul stood still. Seconds later he heard the angry beat of rotor blades.

"Come on," Monica hissed, tugging at his arm.

Up ahead, Paul could see the bridge spanning the canal. The helicopter's pulse thumped through the mist, as if from all directions. He staggered up the steeply arched bridge, his feet slipping against the planks. It seemed the helicopter would break through right overhead. On the other side of the canal, he threw open the door of a derelict house. Pigeons panicked all around him, fluttering to sagging rafters, lifting through large gaps in the ceiling.

Just inside, he sank to the floor, peering back out into the mist. "Can you see it?"

The rhythm of the rotor blades was gradually slowing, the noise duller.

"I think it's landed," she said. "On some other pier maybe."

Paul looked toward the hulk. "We can run for it."

"What about Decks?"

"I don't trust him. I've got to get there before he does, before anyone does." He suddenly felt exhausted, but he had to get up, had to move. He would not let his body fail him.

"Look," Monica said in a whisper.

He followed her gaze to the hulk's deck. There was scarcely a silhouette against the bright mist: a thin figure standing near the prow, bony arms taut against the railing. A large head rested atop a spindly neck. The figure turned and moved across the deck, disappearing down a hatchway. It was a stick figure in the distance, but Paul couldn't mistake it. Sam.

Still no sign of him.

The floor of the passageway was slanted slightly, and Paul kept his balance by pushing off the wall with his hand every few seconds. Beams of light shafted through the cracks. After the cool of the morning, the hulk was surprisingly hot and foul smelling. There was a faint but constant ring in his ears.

"I can hear it," he whispered. "The water."

Monica nodded. "We must be so close."

The corridor opened out into a deep chamber. Chains and iron manacles dangled from the walls. Bits of straw lay scattered about among tattered blankets and broken wooden spoons and plates. Something thick and fast brushed his ankle, and he looked down to see a rat scuttling into a hole.

"This must be where they kept the convicts," Monica whispered. She'd paused, her eyes lingering over every corner of the huge room.

"There's no one here," he said impatiently. "Let's go."

"I'm looking for someone, too, Paul," she said with a new dangerous hardness in her voice.

"I'm sorry." He nodded. Of course he wasn't the only one looking. But not ten minutes ago he'd seen his brother on the deck! How could she expect him to slow down now?

"You think she's still alive?"

"Maybe. It's not just that."

"What else?"

"The water," she said softly. "I want to know about the water."

He didn't have time to reply. A shadow flickered across the doorway at the far end of the room, and he was already moving toward it.

"Sam!" he hissed. "It's me."

By the time he reached the doorway, the figure was slipping out of sight around a corner. He broke into a run, heedless of the weak planking that groaned beneath his feet. He turned down another passageway, and there was Sam again, closer this time, but still ahead of him, rushing weightlessly on.

"It's me—Paul!"

It was just like the first night he'd arrived in Watertown, chasing Sam along the rooftops. Why didn't he stop? Couldn't he hear him? Didn't he recognize his voice? Or maybe he just didn't want to stop.

As Sam disappeared past a doorway, Sked stepped out of the shadows right beside him. Paul flinched in surprise. He'd come so far! He wouldn't be held back now, not by some safety-pinned punk! Had Sked seen Sam? Did he know he was on the hulk? Then Paul saw the long knife in Sked's hand, and his frustration gave way to fear.

"Have a nice swim?" asked Monica. "You're back so soon."

Paul could hear the faint tremor in her voice.

"Shut up," said Sked, pushing her roughly against the wall. He took a few steps back, lazily swiping the blade of the knife from Paul to Monica, smiling. Paul felt every tendon and muscle in his body cranked tighter, second by second. So this is how it ends, he thought. Slaughtered against the wall of a half-sunken ship.

"Nice try with the torched boat," said Sked, "but you're not dead yet. I'd do you both right now, but there's some people who want to see you first." He waved the knife down the passageway. "Walk. I'm right behind."

Paul fell into step beside Monica, all his

senses drawn to the spot where the blade might enter his back. He thought of all the films he'd seen where the hero simply spun around and knocked the weapon out of the villain's hand. What a load of crap.

He wondered whether it was just his fear, or if it was getting hotter as they were marched down the passageway. The noise, he was sure, was louder than before—an annoying buzz, like an insect circling his head. They reached a door.

"Open it," Sked told him.

Paul pushed the oak door wide open. A powerful wave of heat washed over him, and the buzzing doubled in intensity. Monica winced, shaking her head as if trying to dislodge the sound. His eyes were immediately pulled to the bright orange glow of flames in an iron furnace. To the left was a thick pipe of corrugated metal, which curved up from the floor and dribbled water into a vat. To the right of the furnace were wooden tables holding electronic equipment, pulsing faint red and green light. Two men were hunched over a table, studying something. They turned as Paul and Monica were ushered in.

"Oh, good," said one blandly.

Paul could only stare. They looked so ordinary, these two Cityweb men. They could have been clerks, stamping documents, listlessly filling in forms. They could have been suburban fathers—maybe they were. One had a slight belly pushing against his shirt; the other wore cheap polyester pants bagging over white sneakers. They looked so harmless. Paul felt sick.

"So this is Samuel's brother."

The voice came from the shadows at the far end of the room. It sounded like cracking joints, a dry grating of bones. Paul squinted into the darkness but made out nothing except a faint smudge of movement.

"There's a certain likeness," came the voice again. "If this one were to be stripped bare." The pitch of the pervasive droning deepened, and a shape emerged into the light.

Mosquito. That was the first thought that pierced the white noise in his head. The bone-pale arms and legs were little more than insect filaments, with elbows and knees that looked bulbous even though they couldn't have been any bigger than golf balls. It was impossible to tell what sex it was; the body was so wizened, clothed only in a few tatters of cloth around its hips. Its skeletal torso throbbed rhythmically, as if in sync with a heartbeat, and Paul could clearly make out the tracery of blood vessels and veins beneath the skin. But there also seemed to be veins over the skin—bundles of thin, transparent tubing twined around the creature's arms and legs, chest and neck, pricking into the flesh. A clear liquid oozed through the tubes, circulating and recirculating, and he knew there was not an ounce of blood in this thing's body—only dead water. He looked up at its head and was momentarily transfixed by the milky-white eyes, which bounced back light so they seemed to focus on everything at once. Even though it was skull-like, fleshless, he could unmistakably see Decks in it.

Where was Sam? What had they done to him? Everything was collapsing around him now. It was like one of his brother's huge war games— if you looked away or didn't keep up well enough, everything changed on you, the whole game board, all the rules. Decks had said David would have died months ago. And here he was with two very relaxed Cityweb men and a room full of lab equipment that could only be Sam's. Nothing made any sense. He was surprised to feel an aching disappointment through his panic: this was not what he had expected. He had wanted to find Sam here, alone, to talk.

David Sturm took three rapid steps toward Paul and then stood absolutely still.

"Yes, he's pure," he told the two Cityweb men, "wonderfully pure. But the other one has water in her." He flicked a skeletal hand in

Monica's direction. "You're not a drinker, are you? No, the hum's too faint. Your parents must have been Waterdrinkers, then, leaving their traces? That's right, isn't it?" Sturm paused, his head angled pensively. "I recognize you."

Monica's body was rigid. "My mother's here, isn't she?"

"So many came here," said Sturm, almost absentmindedly.

"She came here to drink your water, eight months ago."

"Then she's dead," said Sturm simply.

Monica stared ahead, without words, but Paul could feel her grief washing over him like the heat from the furnace.

"She would have been very eager to drink it," Sturm went on. "Happy to take the chance. All of them were. It was an exciting time."

"What is it?" she asked darkly. "The water. Tell me."

And it was only then that Paul heard her voice crack with rage. "You tell me what it is, you stinking freak!"

"It's a mistake."

Sam's voice crept invisibly out of the shadows, and Paul's body filled with joy. He involuntarily took a few steps in the direction of his brother's voice.

"Stay where you are!" Sked snapped behind him.

Sam's voice hung tantalizingly in the air. "Can't you come out where I can see you?" Paul asked.

"Not now," said Sam, his voice coming from a different location.

"Are you okay?"

"The source is here, Paul. I found it."

There was something disturbing about his voice, Paul thought, a cold detachment he'd never heard before.

"What do you mean, it's a mistake?" asked Monica insistently.

"A terrible, wonderful mistake," Sam replied from the darkness. "Twenty years ago, the City launched a pollution cleanup program, much like the one they're working on now. They designed a microorganism, a primitive version of the garbage gobbler I was testing at the university. But this earlier one was a secret. They wanted to test it on-site. They sent divers down and dropped a canister right here, underneath Rat Castle.

"When the pollution didn't break down around the harbor, the City abandoned the project. But something happened to the garbage gobblers. I got hold of the bioengineering templates at the university. I think they must have reacted with

147

some radioactive trace elements in the water. It caused a chain of mutations. It keeps regenerating itself down there, right below our feet. That's what made the water turn. That's what's changed us."

"Garbage, then," said Monica. "Pollution in our veins!"

Paul looked at her, alarmed by the self-loathing in her voice.

"A gift," rasped David Sturm angrily.

"We have uses for it," said the Cityweb man with the white sneakers. "Your brother's developing a refined strain of the water. We're very interested in its applications."

A row of machines emitted a series of sharp beeps, and Paul heard the furnace flaring.

"It won't be much longer now," said Sam. "We'll have the first canister within twelve hours."

"Sam, please let me see you," Paul said, trying to stave off panic.

There was no answer.

"What the hell's going on, Sam?" he shouted.

"Shackle both of them," Sturm told the two Cityweb men. "Take them below to one of the isolation cells. Give them a taste of how my ancestors lived in Rat Castle."

12

THICK METAL HOOPS had been shackled to his ankles and wrists, chaining him to the wall. He couldn't shift his body more than a foot in any direction. He thrashed against the manacles, but the ancient iron links held tight. Beside him, in the pitch-blackness, he could hear Monica going through the same pointless motions, cursing under her breath. His muscles ached with exhaustion.

"Why lock us up? Why didn't they just kill us?"

"They don't want us dead yet, or Sked would have done it in the passage. They're planning something."

"They've got Sam."

"It sounds like they're all working together.

They said he was refining it for them."

"He can't be helping them." But there was no conviction in his words. He had no idea what was going on. It was like some horrible math problem, too many variables, too many possible answers.

"Decks, Armitage—they'll come looking for us, won't they?" he said.

"If they do, they might be joining us down here."

The walls and floorboards were wet, beads of sticky water oozing from the joints. They were probably below the waterline, in a cell in the deep hold of a slowly sinking ship. He reached out, touching hands with her in the darkness.

"I'm sorry about your mom."

"I wanted to know for sure. Now I do."

"She didn't know what she was doing." He wanted to comfort her and wished he could see her face.

"She had a choice. Maybe not toward the end but closer to the beginning. She didn't have to keep drinking it—if she'd cared more."

"She cared," he said, not knowing if that was the right thing to say. He wondered if even now, in the darkness, she was trying to control her expression. "I'm sure she cared a lot."

"He's hardly human, is he, David Sturm? All because of some junk in the water. When I looked at him, I couldn't believe we had the same thing inside us."

"It's not the same," Paul told her gently. "It's not the same at all. And you don't drink it. You never have."

"But I've wanted to!" she said angrily, pulling away her hand. "I lied when I said I didn't. So many times I've almost done it, guzzled it into me! Just to see what it was Mom felt. Maybe you're right, Paul; maybe she couldn't help it. But it was in her; it's in me! I'm just like her!"

"No! You're not responsible for what your mother did!"

"It's inevitable. Before long, I'll start drinking the water, too!"

"You won't! It doesn't work like that." He had no idea if he was right, but what else could he say? He had to convince her—himself, too.

"I don't know if I loved her," she said, "or just wanted to love her. But I don't want to be like her, Paul. I don't."

He pushed himself across the planking as far as his chains would allow. "Come close."

Their mouths barely met. He could feel her tears on his face. He shut his eyes, wanting to lose himself in her warmth, drink her taste into him. Her tongue brushed lightly against his, and his whole body glowed. He could feel one of her hands knotted through his hair, and he wanted her to pull at it, pull as hard as she could, hurt him if need be, to bring them as close together as possible. And he had it again—the whole world collapsed into the feel of her mouth against his, the smell of her hair.

When a muscle cramped in his neck, he winced and laughed at the same time. He kneaded his neck clumsily with a manacled hand. "Wow, that really hurt."

"You thought I was a freak when you first came," she said reflectively.

"No," he said, surprised and guilty.

She chuckled quietly. "Come on, I could tell. I was ugly to you."

"Never ugly—just different, I guess. I'd never seen a girl like you in Governor's Hill."

"I've been up there, you know." ·

"You were?"

"Once, a few years back. I wanted to have a look. Everyone had these perfect lawns. You could see lines where they unrolled the grass."

Paul smiled in the darkness of the cell. Governor's Hill now seemed a very long time ago.

"I went to a mall," she said. "The girls were pretty. They looked a little plastic, most of them, but I wished I was more like them. So I pickpocketed a couple, came back home. I was so angry at

Mom for drinking the water, for making me a freak."

"You're not," said Paul. "You're very beautiful." He'd never said that before.

She touched his hand. "Thank you. But it's not just the outside, Paul." She sighed. "I could build the biggest gate in the world, run my life with perfect control, but Mom'd still be inside me, running through my veins. And I'll never be free of her."

Paul thought achingly of Sam. They didn't look like brothers; their blood and bodies were completely different, but Paul felt more bound to him than if they'd been identical twins. When he looked in the mirror, sometimes he saw his brother gazing back.

"I worry," said Monica, "that I might be like Sam."

"What do you mean?"

"I don't know what's going to happen to us—anyone who had Waterdrinker parents. I think we might have shortened lives, too."

"No," he told her fiercely. "No!"

Her fingers tightened around his in a grip that was almost painful.

The creak of a door woke him with a start. He could make out a thin silhouette slipping into the cell and crouching against the opposite wall.

"You awake?"

"Sam?"

"I didn't think you'd come, Paul. I really didn't."

"You kept running away—at Jailer's Pier and that night at the stilt house. Why?"

"I didn't want you to see me. You would have been shocked. That's why I left the diskette for you at the boathouse."

"You left it?" But his surprise quickly wore off. Of course. Sam was too exacting to leave something by accident. But Paul found it a little unnerving all the same, as if he'd fallen unknowingly into the steel grooves of some perfect strategy in one of Sam's board games. Sam watching him, leaving clues for him to find, while Paul looked for him in desperation.

"Can I see you now?" he asked nervously.

A pale flashlight beam washed down the far wall. Paul squinted. He supposed he'd been expecting something far worse, something with tubes. But he was only concentrating on Sam's face, afraid of what he might see if he looked lower. It was still recognizable, still Sam. The hollows of his cheeks were slightly deeper, the thin, black hair a little longer. His blue eyes seemed duller than Paul remembered, and he thought of

Sturm's eyes, cataract white, without pupils or color. As he stared, his vision seemed to contract, and everything else around him disappeared. For a few moments he actually forgot about his chains.

"It's good to see you," he whispered.

Now he let his eyes slide down from his brother's face. The skin that showed through his tattered T-shirt and jeans was skeleton-white, and Paul could see the angles and planes of bones and ribs, alarmingly close to the surface. A dream image glittered dully in his mind—Sam lifting his shirt, *Paul, watch*.

"What's happened, Sam?" Beside him, Monica shifted in her sleep; Paul glanced over, worried that their voices might wake her. He wanted to be alone with Sam.

"Don't worry," his brother said. "She needs deep sleep for a few hours. She's been running off of the water for too long. She won't wake up."

"When did they catch you?" Paul asked.

"They didn't. We caught them. They were using infrared scanning from their helicopter. They must have picked up the ship's furnace. When they set down in Rat Castle, Sturm could feel them coming. We surprised them, took away their guns, shackled them. Sturm's very powerful with the water now, very fast."

"He was supposed to be dead."

"Not dead—sleeping. He'd managed to give himself a total transfusion of the water, and that put him into a coma. The water was still contaminated. I gave him a partial transfusion of the filtered water I'd been using, and he came out of it."

His brother's voice was detached, clinical. He could have been talking to a stranger.

"Sturm had been trying to refine the water for years," Sam went on. "Superheating—that was his method. At first I thought it was laughable, like alchemists, lead into gold. But after a few tests, I could see that he was onto something. I've found a way to refine it, Paul. It's very time-consuming and doesn't produce much. But it makes the water infinitely more powerful. I'm the only one who knows how to do it. Sturm needs me. And the Cityweb men need me, too."

"For what?"

"They're not stupid. After they found my working notes in the lab, they did their homework. They think it's worth a lot of money."

"And you're helping them?"

"The water belongs to Sturm. He'll kill anyone who tries to steal it. He came to an agreement with them. I think it's stupid—I don't trust them— but the two Cityweb guys say they'll buy the refined water from him and sell it in the City."

"A new drug?"

"In small doses, it should give you a short burst of exhilaration, heightened awareness, speed, strength." Sam chuckled darkly. "I'm sure it's going to be very popular. But I'm refining it for myself, please understand that—for my own experiments."

"I thought they'd kill you," said Paul. He wanted to break through the icy crust of his brother's voice: It's me, remember me? Talk to me. "I was sure they would kill you." He felt he might cry. "They were looking for you when I came."

"Not me, Paul. You."

"What do you mean?"

"They came to Rat Castle almost a week ago."

"What about Sked—he was looking for you."

Sam shook his head. "Sked was out of touch, didn't know they'd found me."

"But look, last night on the boat, he tried to kill us!"

"No, Cityweb had caught up with him by then. He was only supposed to bring you here."

Paul was panicky now. "It's because I read the diskette, isn't it?"

"They want to use you, Paul. You're uncontaminated. Pure."

Sturm's words sounded in his head. *He's pure,*

157

wonderfully pure. Paul was suddenly aware of an icy chill seeping through his whole body.

"They want to test the refined water on you."

"No." His voice was barely audible.

"They'll kill you if you won't let them."

"I won't take any of that crap inside me!"

"It's not dangerous; I can guarantee that. And the doses will be too small to be addictive. I'll administer them myself."

He stared in disbelief. "You want me to do this, don't you?" Things started slipping into place: the phone call, the arranged meeting, the diskette left for him to find at the boathouse. He thought of Sam in the ship's passageway, leading him toward Sturm and Cityweb.

"You knew all along, didn't you, Sam?"

"It wasn't my idea."

"You lured me here for them!"

"They said they'd cut me off from the water if I didn't. I had no choice."

No choice. Wasn't that Armitage's explanation, too? *I had no choice.* And Monica's mother. She'd had no choice either—he'd said so himself, to soothe Monica.

"You betrayed me, Sam."

"'Let's see what he looks like without his clothes on,'" Sam recited the words slowly, carefully. "'His shirt . . . his jeans.'"

Paul could barely swallow. "How did you know?"

"Randy's friends were talking about it in the hallways—too stupid to keep their mouths shut about how they were all going to meet, and wait for me after school. Randy knew where I'd be. And Randy knew where I'd be . . . ," his voice trailed off, as though he were actually savoring the memory—"because you knew where I'd be."

"I told them not to touch you," Paul said quickly, desperate now to explain. "Randy promised me. He was just supposed to scare you—"

"You were a fool to believe him."

"I know."

He had no words now. Any apology would be hollow. But there was a spark of hope, a glimpse of something shared, something that might bring them together.

"Why did you do that to me, Paul?"

"Because I hated you!" The words were hot and unexpected and euphoric. "I hated you because you were leaving home and you didn't care that I was going to be left behind. That wasn't the way it was supposed to be, Sam! We were supposed to stay together. We made plans, remember? You once told me I was nothing without you. And you were right. But I never said you were nothing without me. I wanted to show you!

You still needed me!"

He'd been straining against the chains, and now he slumped back, breathing hard. "It was wrong what I did."

"You were the only person I trusted," came Sam's measured reply, and with a sick heart, Paul knew the moment was over. "And when you set me up, you convinced me of what I always knew deep down. That you can only rely on yourself. I needed you once, Paul," said Sam, standing. "But not now, not anymore."

From his bed, he heard his parents' voices drifting down the hallway: his father's, low and even, punctuated by his mother's, sharp with her hissing s's. He could never make out the exact words, but it was impossible for him to sleep while they were fighting. He rolled onto his back, gazing up at the ceiling. Whenever this happened, he invented games to distract himself. Bicycling his legs in the air until they ached, naming countries.

His door opened, letting in a crack of light. Sam slipped into the room, shutting the door softly behind him.

"You awake?"

"Yep."

"They're fighting."

"I know."

Sam sat down on the edge of the bed. Paul knew he was waiting to be asked.

"You want to get in?"

"All right."

Paul moved over and Sam slipped under the covers.

"It never seems as dark in your room," Sam said. "It's good." They lay there in silence for a few moments, side by side. Paul was always amazed at how much heat his brother's tiny body gave off, like some whirring electric dynamo. He could still hear the voices.

"You want to make a fort?"

"Yeah," said Sam enthusiastically. He loved forts. Together they scooted down under the covers, creating a cave of blankets and sheets. There was no sound except for their own breathing.

"What do they fight about?" Sam asked from the darkness. "Maybe they wanted to watch different TV programs." They both giggled.

"Maybe it's money," said Sam.

"No. We've got lots of money."

"It's me, then."

"No it's not."

"Yesterday, when we came out of the doctor's, Mom yelled at me."

"She was just tired. You want to listen to the radio?"

"Okay."

Paul leaned out from the covers into the cool of the room and grabbed the small transistor radio. Back inside their fort, he turned the round switch on the side of the radio. There was a familiar squelch of static, and the light came on behind the tuner.

They rolled through the stations, listening to scraps of news broadcasts, rock, big-band music. Then Paul found a comedy about a giant fish: there were exaggerated voices and funny sound effects. The giant fish was upsetting boats and terrorizing people. An old fisherman hooked it from the bridge, but the fish was so big the whole bridge came down.

They were giggling under the covers, sticking their heads out every once in a while to gulp in some fresh air.

"You sleepy?" Paul asked when the play was over.

"Uh-huh."

Paul made out the sharp contours of Sam's body, sprawled out, his head on a pillow, eyes closed.

"You going back to your room?"

"Yeah," came the muffled reply. He didn't move, faking sleep.

"Well, you can stay here if you want." Paul

tried to sound reluctant. No answer. Smiling to himself, Paul turned over on his side and went to sleep.

"You were crying in your sleep," Monica said, stirring beside him.

"I wasn't asleep." He'd been wide awake since Sam left. He scrubbed away his tears with the back of his hand. "I was thinking about when we were little kids. He came down here while you were sleeping."

"He did?"

"He's helping them—you were right. They want to test the water on me."

Monica just stared, speechless. Her hands were trembling. "We're going to get out of here, Paul."

He felt as if he were peering down at himself from a great height. "He said he stopped trusting me after what I did to him. People are unreliable, he said. You know what? He sounded exactly like you." He shivered, suddenly cold.

"Paul, look—"

"So maybe he's right. You were both right. I came down here thinking I could fix things between us, my head full of all this junk I might say, stuff out of greeting cards. It was a waste of time." He clenched his teeth. "He doesn't need me anymore."

"Paul, he's gone crazy with the water."

He felt hollow, like some gutted machine slumped in a junk heap.

"We're getting out of here," she said fiercely. "Give me your belt."

"What for?"

"I might be able to use the pin to pick these locks."

He made a halfhearted attempt to reach his belt with his manacled hands. "Can't do it."

"Try again."

"There's no point."

"Paul, give me the belt!"

Even in the near dark he could see the flash of her tears. "Don't do this, Paul. Please don't give up like this. Give me the belt. I need you to do this for me. I need you."

He stretched out his arms as far as the chains would allow, but his hands still couldn't quite reach the belt. He was disgusted by his self-pity. He arched his back, wrenching his hips up higher, grunting with the effort.

With two fingers he caught the end of the belt and tried to pull it loose. The strain was too much. He had to rest. He tried again; this time the pin popped out of the belt. He flicked the pin away so it wouldn't snag in any of the other holes and slowly pulled away the buckle.

"Good, you're doing it," said Monica.

He took another rest before taking hold of the belt and starting to ease it through the loops in his jeans. It slid out smoothly at first, then caught halfway. He yanked hard, and his jeans bunched up around the waist. He took a deep breath, trying to ignore the hot pain in his armpits and lower back, and with gentle tugs pulled the belt through the rest of the way.

He handed it over to Monica and sank back, sweating. He couldn't watch her as she worked, clutching the pin between two slender fingers and bending her wrist, almost to snapping, to fiddle with the keyhole in the manacle. Her neck was twisted up and around so she could catch a glimpse of what she was doing. Sometimes the pin slipped out, and it took a long time to get it back into the keyhole; other times, she gave up with a growl of rage. But she always went back to it.

Finally, there was a metal clink, and the first manacle popped open, releasing Monica's right hand. She was pale with the effort.

"That's one," she panted. "I've never done locks before. The others should be faster."

Paul heard the sound of a bolt being shot back in the cell door. Monica quickly put her wrist back in the manacle. The door creaked open

13

"**H**OW DOES IT feel to be shackled?"

On deck, Paul shuddered in the night air. Without speaking a word, Sam had unlocked the chains that tethered him to the wall, leaving his wrists and legs manacled. "Where are we going?" Paul had asked as he shambled through the doorway, guided by Sam's viselike grip. But Sam made no reply. Paul was afraid, but what he felt most was utter loneliness. At least Sam hadn't noticed Monica's unlocked manacle or the belt, which she'd shoved behind her back.

"I've been shackled all my life," Sam went on, "inside my body, rotting away."

Paul looked around the deck, confused. He'd assumed he was being led back to the forge, to

Sturm and the Cityweb men. But he and Sam were alone.

"Look how strong I am now!" Sam cried out. He darted to the ship's railing, ripping away thick wooden struts, heaving them into the water.

"And look how high I can jump!"

Paul watched Sam leap into the air, to the top of the severed mast, dangling from the jagged tip by his fingers, then letting himself fall slowly to the ground, landing lightly on two feet, knees barely bending.

"I'm stronger than you now, Paul. Faster, too."

Paul frowned. A part of him couldn't accept this. It was Sam who had always been the weak one, not him. Sam had the brains, Paul the strength. It wasn't right that Sam now had both. It made Paul redundant.

"You want to arm wrestle, Paul? I think I'll hold out longer than last time! I'll try not to twist your wrist off."

"Why'd you bring me up here?"

"You know me better than anyone else."

Paul thought there was a pleading quality in his voice, but he tried to block it out, wishing he felt nothing.

"There're some things I need to tell you," said Sam, again almost confidingly. "I want you to understand why I'm doing this."

"You hated your body; you always did."

"But you never truly knew what it was like. You probably think the worst thing was the humiliation of getting bullied, my helplessness, my hatred of the Randy Smiths of this world. But the worst of it was the guilt."

Paul stared in astonishment.

"The guilt of needing to be protected, needing to be taken care of, needing special attention, needing pills—always, always needing! But worst of all, the guilt that I'd failed myself. Every time I went to the doctor's, they weighed me. It seems like such a simple thing, doesn't it? But I was sweating when I stepped onto that scale. They'd adjust the weights, starting high, and work down, down, down. The numbers were the same almost every time, maybe a few pounds lighter, but never heavier. I felt responsible: it was my fault. Somehow, there was something I wasn't doing right! And the nurses and doctors would look at me, look at the weight on the scales, then write the number in my file: silent, invisible blame."

"It's just not true. How could it be your fault? It's nobody's fault."

"Ah, but it doesn't work that way, does it? You blamed me, too, Paul."

Paul was about to protest, but he faltered, remembering his reaction when Sam told him he wasn't going to live a full life. He'd felt pity, grief, but revulsion, too—a drawing away, an angry pointing of the finger. *This is your fault.*

"And Mom and Dad weren't any different," Sam went on. "They wanted me to get better—I really do believe that. They took me to the best doctors they knew, spent hours with me in hospitals. But I wasn't performing—that's the way they thought of it. I could see it in their silences, the way I caught them looking at me sometimes. They were putting x into me, but I wasn't putting y out—like some math equation! When it came right down to it, I was an embarrassment, their failure. They were glad when I left for college. It was a big sigh of relief for them."

Sam paused, wiping a hand across his mouth. Paul realized with a start that he felt strangely happy; there was something connecting them again. Sam needed him—even if it was just as an audience.

"With the refined water," Sam said, "I'll finally be able to heal myself. On the diskette, I said I was hyperaware of my body's structure. Now I can start to focus on specific groups of cells. Soon I'll be able to control them individually. Didn't you ever find it incredible that millions of things go on in your body without you even knowing? Only the body knows how to do these things.

But now I'm linked up. I'll witness all the sub-atomic secrets scientists and doctors have been theorizing about for decades. I'll be able to repair all the damage that was done to me before I was even born!"

"But how?" Paul wanted to know, mistrustful of the unwieldy excitement in Sam's voice. "Tubes into your veins? Let all the blood out, so that you look like Sturm?"

Sam shook his head, a condescending smile on his lips. "Sturm's totally dependent on the water. Interrupt the flow and he'd be dead in minutes. He's a slave. I need to take a huge amount of the refined water all at once. And in that single burst of awareness—that's when I'll be able to do the work with my mind. A bloodless operation, Paul."

"An overdose."

Sam shrugged. "I wouldn't have used that term."

"I'm afraid for you. I'm afraid you're going to kill yourself."

"No. I'm going to make myself perfect."

Paul thought of Leonardo da Vinci's perfect man—Sam's version, the one whose body was half machine. In his head he heard the oiled push of steel pistons, the rustle of rubber hosing. He heard the low roar of a powerful furnace and realized it

was the sound of a steel heart pumping relent-
lessly, flawlessly, without feeling.

"Perfect," Paul said, his voice almost a whisper. "What does that mean, Sam? That your body
will never give out? You won't get a cold, you won't
get cancer? You'll live longer? Who wouldn't want
all that? But you're more interested in being a
machine than a human being."

Sam smiled. "Like you, Paul."

"What?"

"Strip!"

Paul could only stare in bewilderment.

Sam violently tore open Paul's shirt. "Show
me your muscles!"

How often Sam used to ask that. *Show me
your muscles.* But there was a savageness in his
request now—a hatred.

"Come on, flex!" Sam shouted. "You know
the position, Paul! You did it every night in front
of the mirror. Arms up and out, legs spread, chest
swelled. Do it for me now! Da Vinci's perfect
man! You loved that power. You loved the power it
gave you over others, over me! You worshipped
that machine power of your body, labored over it,
honed it!"

Paul felt his whole body shaking; he couldn't
breathe. Something was tangled in his guts,
wedged in his throat, as if Sked were choking him

again. Then all at once it broke through, and he was sobbing.

Sam was right. The truth had been staring back into his eyes—his reflection in the mirror, his own image of perfection. He'd been so vain, so stupid. Why hadn't he seen it in Watertown, where he was weak; he broke things, fell behind, needed babysitting.

All the time he'd searched for Sam, he'd been telling himself to stay strong, as if for some epic track event, as if finding Sam were a physical feat. He thought of his fight with Sked; it had left him sick and frightened of what he could make his body do.

But beneath the muscle, he was eggshell frail. He thought of Monica and her big iron gate, trying to stay in perfect control so nothing could get close enough to hurt her. And Armitage, hoping to build his own perfect empire on revenge. All their pathetic ideas of perfection.

"I still need you, Paul."

Paul almost laughed through his tears; the idea was so ludicrous and so cruel.

"Do you know why I called you?" Sam's voice was gentler now, almost apologetic. "It wasn't to set you up. I phoned you before Cityweb found me. I called you because I wanted you down here, to show you what I'd found. I had a plan."

"Yeah, what was that?"

"You've got one wish."

The familiar words, the start of the game.

"Only this time," said Sam, "we share a wish, because it's for both of us. I know what your wish is. It's mine, too. Shall I say it?"

Paul swallowed hard and nodded.

"I want us to be equals again." He paused, then said, "Take the water with me, Paul."

His words hung in the air, still whispering.

"Put us together, and we really could have been something, huh?" Sam said.

Paul smiled weakly. But he was remembering when he'd looked into the mirror, past his brother, and seen their bodies welded together. Even then he had known they were complementary, insepa-rable.

"I'll teach you how to use the water, Paul. Sturm's killing himself. He thinks a transfusion of the refined water will make him even stronger, but it's burning his body away. A month, that's the most he has. It'll be just you and me, Paul—our rules, our place."

Our fort—it was being held out to him. *Here, take it.* He would never have to worry about Sam leaving him again. He could have everything back the way it was. Was this the perfection he'd wanted all along? But there was a persistent shimmering at the back of his mind.

"Monica," he said, as if talking in his sleep.

"She's a problem, Paul. They were planning on killing both of you after the tests. I can bargain for you, Paul, but—"

"I want her safe, too."

Sam sighed impatiently. "Paul, she's got the water in her. She doesn't have more than five years before it starts burning her down."

"No—" He'd told her she'd be all right, that she wouldn't end up like her mother.

"I'm sorry," said Sam, "but it's the truth. I've got all the data."

"But you can help her! Can't you?"

"Paul. Forget about her. Remember what's important. You and me!"

He'd forget about her, wouldn't he? How long had he known her? A few days, no more. He'd known Sam almost a lifetime. So just one more betrayal, that's all it would take. A quick nod of his head. And then? He would drink the refined water with Sam, and they would become perfectly equal. He would never need a mirror again, because Sam would reflect his own perfect image back at him.

He sucked in his breath, as if in pain. His head cleared. It was selfish. It was utter loneliness. And it would never be enough.

"Let's leave. Together," Paul said. "Right now."

"Listen to me! I've been working toward this moment for years. I'm almost finished. Besides, where would I go, Paul? Back to Governor's Hill? Like this? Look at me. I'm a freak, a horror. What would the neighbors say? Say I stopped taking the water, say there were no aftereffects. How many years do I have? Twelve, if I'm lucky? It's not enough! Stay, take the water with me!"

"I can't do it, Sam." He had to force himself to say the words.

"You owe me this!"

In Sam's voice, Paul thought he heard a very small child, resentful, bitter, raging. The same boy that was in him, too. He'd hated Sam when he'd left home; he needed Sam too much.

He had to turn away. "I'm sorry, Sam."

The movement was so sudden Paul recoiled in shock. Sam grasped the shackles around his wrists, buckling the metal with his fingers. He then dropped to his knees, breaking his ankle chains.

"Leave, then."

Paul hesitated.

"Get Monica out, and leave." Sam threw a ring of keys at his feet. "But you do it without me!"

"Sam, please!" He was in agony. How could

he just leave, knowing what Sam was going to do? He seized his brother's arm. "Come with us!"

But Sam gave him a punch in the face that sent him sprawling, a grunt of surprise still locked in his throat.

"My work here isn't finished yet!"

Paul touched his cheekbone in amazement.

"Get going!" Sam said. "Before I change my mind."

"Wait, listen—" But Sam punched him again, hard.

"All right then, let's fight."

They squared off. Paul didn't know why he was doing this; he knew he'd lose. He made a half-hearted lunge, which his brother easily avoided, jabbing him under the chin. Paul staggered back, dizzy. He was a ninety-pound weakling getting sand kicked in his face.

He pushed himself forward, hoping to knock Sam over, but his brother darted effortlessly behind him, pinning his arms against his sides. Paul writhed to get free, but Sam held him in the steel hoops of his arms.

"This is important," Sam breathed against his ear. "I need to do this for myself."

"You don't," Paul choked. "Let me go! Come with us!"

"No."

Sam's grip loosened slightly, just enough so that it no longer hurt. Paul could feel their bodies moving in tandem as they both gasped for breath. He could feel the faint tremor of his brother's pulse beating against his back. And Paul suddenly knew Sam wasn't fighting with him anymore. He was hugging him, holding him fiercely in his arms.

"Go!"

Paul whirled around, but Sam had already disappeared.

14

HE SHOULD HAVE paid more attention earlier. Which way? Right or straight ahead? What if she'd picked the other locks, set herself free? She might have left the ship already. He tried to think straight. He'd have to go back to the cell to make sure. But Sam. How could he leave him here? He felt bruised where he'd been hugged.

The canted floors sent him teetering against the walls. Up ahead, thick crossbeams sagged precariously from the low ceiling, forcing him to stoop to get past. He remembered this part. A map was drawing itself in his head. Down another set of steps and he'd almost be there.

On the lower deck, he felt along the wall in near darkness. There. The door. He fumbled with the keys. It took him three tries to make the match. He flung the door open and rushed inside. With a surge of relief, he made out Monica's shape against the wall.

"Sam's letting us go," he whispered, touching her skin.

It felt hard, icy cold. Bone, plastic tubing. The insect hum welled up around him, deafening.

"I thought you'd come back for her," said David Sturm.

The stench of rot wafted over him. Smell of death, he thought in terror. Sturm was dying, like Sam said. Dying from the inside out. Before Paul had time to move, bone-thin hands latched onto his shoulders, and he was lifted to his feet. Sturm's eyes, Paul noticed, were shut tight, but he must have been able to see him in his head, hear the frenzied pumping of his heart, smell the sweat seeping from his skin. He cast a frantic look around the cell.

"Where's Monica?" he demanded in a choked voice.

"Waiting at the furnace. We haven't hurt her."

Not yet.

"I've got a thirst, Paul. And you have to take the first few sips for me. My ancestors watched the lake grow increasingly more foul from the City's contamination. Now I'm going to give the City its dead water back. I'm going to make them beg for the dead water in their veins."

There was a chair, and beside it, a small table.

Paul's eyes picked out a package of sterile swabs, loops of surgical tubing and a neat row of syringes. His stomach lurched, and he thought he was going to be sick.

He saw Monica, chained against a wall to the right of the furnace. Sked hovered nearby, hungrily watching the flames through the window in the iron door—a dog hoping for scraps. The two Cityweb men were studying some equipment, the one with the white sneakers rubbing sleep from his eyes, like a reluctant office worker on a Monday morning.

"We're almost ready."

Sturm forced Paul into the chair, and the Cityweb men locked him in tight, one belt across the legs, another across the chest. He could feel droplets of sweat gathering on his forehead.

"We'll be injecting the water directly into your bloodstream," White Sneakers explained. "Normally the user would drink it, but we think the results will be a little faster this way. Comfortable?"

He spoke like a dentist making small talk

before drilling. For a moment it threw Paul off—
he made it all sound so reasonable, so ordinary.
But then he glanced at Monica, and their eyes
met. He didn't want to be seen like this, strapped
to a chair, needles pricking his skin. And where
was Sam now? Paul imagined him watching from
the shadows with cold detachment.

Sturm lurched to the blast furnace and pulled
on a pair of thick gloves. He pushed up a long
lever to the left of the furnace door. Paul could see
the flames subside behind the window and
instantly felt the heat in the room abate. Sturm
opened the thick iron door, seized a pair of tongs,
and brought out a canister, glowing orange hot.
He set it in a bucket on one of the long tables with
a loud sigh of steam.

"Thirty seconds to cool," said White
Sneakers, looking at his watch.

"Flat out, please," said Beer Belly, easing
Paul's arm down against the chair's armrest. Just
like taking blood.

"Time," announced White Sneakers.

Sturm lifted the canister out of the bucket and
twisted off the lid. There was a sharp hiss of
inrushing air. White Sneakers poked a syringe
inside and eased up the plunger to draw in the
dead water.

Paul flinched as Beer Belly slapped at the

inside of his elbow with two fingers. "Good muscle definition," he said. "I used to do weight training. There we are; that's the vein." He wiped a cool, wet cotton pad over the skin. Paul snapped up his arm. It was completely automatic. He knew they would wrestle him down in the end.

"I need some help here," said Beer Belly placidly. He and White Sneakers grabbed Paul's forearm and started to force it down. It gave him satisfaction to resist—you flabby wimps—but he could feel his strength giving out, his muscles pulpy with fear.

"Let's not waste time," said Sturm. He darted to Monica. One clawlike hand flashed out and closed around Monica's neck. Fury exploded through Paul, and he thrashed around in the chair, smacking Beer Belly in the face with his fist. He wanted to tear at Sturm's insect limbs, gouge thumbs into the milky whites of his eyes.

"She can't breathe!" called out Sturm.

With a groan of despair, Paul stopped struggling, lowered his arm, shut his eyes, tight.

"All right," he whispered. All right, all right. Waiting for the pinprick, waiting for the dead water.

"David!"

Paul opened his eyes and wrenched his head around. Decks stood in the doorway, hands steadying a pistol aimed at Sturm.

Behind him, Armitage hefted a shotgun. "Tim, Bob! Hi, you guys!" he said cheerfully. "Good to know you've been keeping busy since trashing my house. Why don't you just put that needle down and move back against the wall. Do it now! You, too, Sked." He waved the shotgun convincingly. "That's it. Very nice."

"Stand away from the girl, David." Decks slowly walked forward, keeping his aim steady.

"Decks," said Sturm, opening out his arms in a grotesque parody of welcome.

"It's an abomination what you've done here."

"You never understood," said Sturm. "You let yourself become hysterical. It was just jealousy, Decks; we both know that. The water wasn't for you. But that's past now. Look." He pointed to the canister on the table. "We've refined it. Anyone can drink it. You can."

"No, David."

"The family, Decks, you haven't forgotten. We'll make our comeback after all, you and I!"

Paul could see Decks adjusting his grip on the pistol, blinking sweat away from his eyes.

"Don't move."

"Let me embrace you, brother."

David Sturm shambled slowly forward, then all at once broke into a run, his insect drone building in intensity. A pistol shot tore through the air and he was wrenched around, barely an arm's length from Decks. He collapsed to the floor, a small pool of greenish water forming around his shoulder. The hum stopped.

Paul sank back in his chair, limp, and watched as Decks lowered the pistol and stepped cautiously toward his fallen brother.

"There was no other way," he muttered. He looked across at Paul. "We'll have you both out in a second."

The insect hum sounded again, and before Paul could shout a warning, Sturm had snapped upright and latched a quick hand around Decks's forearm. The gun dropped from numb fingers and Decks sank to his knees, his face blank with pain. Sturm rose to his feet, blocking Paul's view, but when he heard the horrible crunch, he was glad he couldn't see what was happening.

He heard Armitage shout in alarm and turned to see him swinging the shotgun around on Sturm. His shot was panicked, and his aim was off, tearing a jagged hole in the chamber's curving wall. The two Cityweb men lunged and toppled Armitage from behind.

It was Sked who snatched up the gun. With a yelp of triumph, he rushed toward Paul. But it was the syringe Sked wanted. He snatched it up in one hand, the shotgun in the crook of his other arm.

Backing against the forge, his eyes danced wildly around the chamber.

"Good work, Sked," said White Sneakers, pinning Armitage to the ground. "Bring it over."

"Been a long time coming," said Sked, looking at the syringe. "This one's for me!"

The spider boy plunged the needle into his arm. Paul stared in horror—everyone, he realized, was waiting to see what would happen. Sked flung the needle aside, chest heaving. His body drooped forward for an instant, then arched back violently.

"Yes!" he roared. "Yes, yes, yes, yes!"

Paul's eyes fixed on the barrel of the shotgun as it swung erratically around the chamber.

"I'm fast!" Sked ranted. "I can feel it! Look at me!" He pummeled the air with his free fist, dodging blows from invisible opponents.

"The gun, Sked!" said Beer Belly. There was, at last, a trace of emotion in his voice—worry this time. "Bring it here."

"'Bring it here, bring it here,'" Sked mimicked in a thick voice. "Who are you guys—ordering me around like—"

"Sked!" White Sneakers was advancing on him like an angry parent. Paul could see that the spider boy had broken into a heavy sweat and his pale face had assumed a demented squint. "You've screwed up enough!"

"Stay away!" Sked bellowed. "Everyone stay away! I'm fast!"

"Give me the gun, Sked!"

The shotgun jumped in Sked's trembling hands. White Sneakers hit the floor, staring at the ceiling, lifeless.

"See, I'm fast!" Sked shrieked his hyena laughter. He skipped across the room and leveled the shotgun at Beer Belly. Armitage disappeared under a table. Another blast, and Beer Belly was driven back against the wall with an annoyed grunt, a red stain spreading across his shirt.

Sturm was across the room in an instant, one hand clasped under Sked's jaw, the other behind his neck. There was a sharp snap and the boy's limp body slid to the boards. Without a pause, Sturm was rushing toward Paul, bony feet scarcely touching the ground. Paul yelled, as if the force of his lungs could repel the skeletal monster. Sturm snatched up a second syringe, filled it, and leaned over him. "Now! Straighten your arm!"

"Don't touch him!"

Paul saw the blur of Sam's body, plummeting from the rafters and catching David Sturm around the shoulders. The two crashed to the floor, a few feet from Paul's chair. Sam clutched a bundle of tubing around Sturm's neck and tore it loose. A fine drizzle tickled Paul's face—

hot, oily—and he spat it away.

Armitage appeared beside him, a ring of keys in his hand, hurriedly unlocking the straps. Paul leaped from the chair.

"Do Monica!" he told Armitage.

Sam and Sturm were locked tight, skeletal limbs smashing out, whirling them closer to the blast furnace. Paul could see his brother's hands wrenching at Sturm's tubes, and a strong jet of water arched across the chamber. Paul flung himself onto Sturm's back, but he was thrown off effortlessly with a jab from a poker-sharp elbow. He slammed against the scalding door of the furnace, winded.

He saw Armitage pulling the shotgun from Sked's limp hands, leveling it.

"No!" Paul shouted hoarsely. "No! They're too close!"

Armitage hesitated. Sturm gripped Sam's head between his hands, viselike. And for a moment, they were motionless, gazing at each other as if hypnotized. Sturm's insect drone faltered for a moment, and one hand came away to pat uselessly at the ruptured tubing around his neck. Green water flooded over his fingers. Sam wrenched himself free.

Sturm's hum deepened and he swayed on his feet. Paul's heart quickened. He struggled upright, his hands feeling behind him, burning against the iron door of the blast furnace. Sturm limped after Sam, arms outstretched. Paul's hands closed around the handle of the door, teeth grinding against the pain. Just a few more steps. All he needed was a few more steps. Now.

He flung open the door and gasped from the heat.

"Sam, get out of the way!"

He pulled the lever hard.

Sturm whirled. For a split second, his skeletal face was bathed in a violent orange glow, and then he was engulfed in a roaring column of flame.

Paul flung his arms over his face, heat scalding his exposed skin. A second blast shot out. He clawed for the lever and managed to push it up into place. But the chamber was already alive with flames, licking against the parched walls, crackling in the high rafters. Water streamed from Paul's eyes as he staggered through the billowing smoke. He nearly tripped over Sturm's blackened skeleton, clenched tight like a fist, hissing steam.

He could hear Monica and Armitage calling out for him, but he lurched across the chamber, his hands stretched in front of him, pelted by a hail of sparks. Through the smoke he could see Sam. Paul called out to him, filled with relief. Sam was holding something in his hands. Paul squinted. It was the canister of refined water. He met his brother's eyes for only a few seconds before losing him in a thick swirl of smoke. When it cleared, Sam was gone.

15

THE HULK WAS burning and sinking.

He staggered to the pier beside Monica and Armitage, watching the flames spread through the ancient ship. He was still coughing smoke from his lungs, spitting soot. His hair and clothing were singed.

Flames twisted up through the deck like some magical plant, sending orange shoots along the planking, buckling timbers, twisting up the broken masts. Tendrils of fire pierced the hull near the waterline, and smoke billowed out. With a mighty groan, the hulk listed sluggishly.

Paul watched, feeling nothing. Burning and sinking at the same time.

* * *

From the stilt-house roof, he could still see the orange glow shimmering above the center of Watertown, black smudges drifting out across the night sky. Monica sat down beside him.

"Can't sleep?" she asked.

"No."

"How are your burns?"

He glanced down at his bandaged hands. "They're fine. You did a good job. Thank you."

They sat in silence for a few minutes.

"I saw Armitage a few hours ago," Paul said, "with a bunch of other guys."

"They went back to Rat Castle to sink the helicopter. Armitage doesn't want any traces."

Paul's eyes scanned the dark outlines of the shantytown. "I wonder where Sam is."

Monica shook her head, smiling sadly.

"He got out all right," Paul said, almost to himself. "We just missed him in all the smoke." He felt only a weary resignation.

"He could be anywhere now," she said.

"Do you think he'll drink it?"

"He might."

"He wanted us to be equals so badly. I wonder if he thinks I betrayed him, because I wouldn't drink the water."

"You were right not to."

"But what about him? Maybe I was asking too

much. Was it wrong for him to want to heal himself?"

"He didn't even know if it would work, Paul. It was a guess, a crazy guess."

"He could still do it, though." He tilted his head back to the night sky, shutting his eyes, wishing he could clear away all his thoughts and sleep. "Maybe that's right for him. Maybe—who knows, he might make some kind of medical breakthrough."

But Monica was shaking her head. "It only ever killed people, Paul. In the end."

He nodded slowly, looking at her. Five years, Sam had said. He twined his burned fingers through hers and gazed back over Watertown.

He found the note at the foot of his bed when he woke late the next morning. It was written on a ripped-out page from a magazine, the cramped words twisting through the white space between advertisements.

I'm not coming back. But you already knew that, I think. I haven't taken the water yet. But I will, and I hope you understand. I was wrong to ask you to drink it with me; you don't owe me anything. What I said about Monica was a lie. I found nothing to prove that the water in her veins would cut short her life. And now I'm going on an adventure, Paul. I hope you wish me well.

    Sam

Paul walked to the window, his body stiff and aching. The sun had almost burned through the morning mist. He suddenly felt filled with light.

Monica bumped the boat against the docklands jetty and idled the motor. She sat looking straight ahead, her hands lightly tapping the wheel.

"Lots of room in our house," she said.

Paul shook his head with a laugh. "I can't."

"Why not?"

"Because I'm not from there." And because I'm a coward, he thought.

He looked across the harbor to Watertown, hazy in the distance. He'd considered staying—forget about Governor's Hill, his parents, school. But he knew he couldn't do it, not yet.

"So when'll you come back down?"

"As soon as I can."

She exhaled noisily, dissatisfied.

"So when will you come up?"

"Never," she said. "Can you see me hanging out at the mall?"

"See, it works both ways."

She nodded reluctantly. "Got everything?"

"Yeah," he said awkwardly. "Thanks." He hefted his knapsack onto his lap.

"You and your stupid knapsack," she said, and suddenly looked away from him.

He leaned across and pressed his face into her hair. As he held her, he knew suddenly that he was falling in love with her, and he drew back, afraid.

"It's not stupid to need people, is it?" he asked her, wanting to be reassured.

"No. It's just that you can get let down."

"How do you know I won't let you down?" he asked.

"I don't," she said simply. "And maybe it doesn't matter."

"No." He knew she was right. All you could do was keep trying.

"Don't wait too long," she said.

"I won't."

He stepped out of the boat and onto the jetty. He felt tentative, a little shaky, as if he'd just recovered from a bad case of flu. But he knew he was very happy. He loved her; he needed her.

He wondered if the whole thing was an impossibility, like some magical gas dissolving in empty air. But he pushed his thoughts ahead to his return. He would stand at the tall gate at the end of the pier, his hands curved around the iron bars, waiting, seeing her walk slowly toward him, to let him in.